Tried not to let her body remember the sensations he'd evoked.

Finding herself on the couch before bed, irritated with television commercials and no longer distracted by movies, Emma pulled out the journal again. Just to see what she'd written.

1. *I want to be loved by a man who loves me so much that my love changes him.*

She stared at the words. She'd written them down because, in that moment, she'd felt them so strongly. Now, days later, she still felt the same way.

She grabbed her pen. WITHDRAWN

2. *I want to be brave enough to live my life to the fullest.*

She read what she'd written again. And reread it several times. If there was going to be any value in this exercise, she had to be completely honest.

And she realized that, like it or not, her resolutions were about Chris....

"Tara Taylor Quinn writes with wonderful assurance and an effective, unpretentious style perfectly suited to her chosen genre." —Jennifer Blake, *New York Times* bestselling author

Dear Reader,

Ever wake up and look at your life and wish some things were different? I have. And sometimes still do. And then what? You shrug and go on with your routine, your day. And most of the time, you're happy. Or at least content.

But what if...

What if *you* decided that the things you wished were different *were* going to be different? What if, instead of shrugging and going on with "normal," you made changes?

What if gets me every time. Meet Emma Sanderson. She's a high school teacher with a mortgage and family responsibilities. She can't just change any of those things in her life. Truth is, she doesn't really want to. She likes teaching and loves her family. But she wants more.

A Daughter's Story is about that *more.* It's about having the courage to make changes where you can—even in small ways. It's about daring to want and to reach for what you want within the realm of who and what you are. It's about taking what you have and doing something to make it even better.

A Daughter's Story is about finding answers. And...as always with me, it's about love.

By the way, I'd really like to know what you think happened to Claire. Write to me at staff@tarataylorquinn.com! And watch for *The Truth About Comfort Cove,* coming in January 2013.

Tara Taylor Quinn

A Daughter's Story

TARA TAYLOR QUINN

HARLEQUIN®
entertain, enrich, inspire™

Recycling programs
for this product may
not exist in your area.

ISBN-13: 978-0-373-60735-8

A DAUGHTER'S STORY

Copyright © 2012 by Tara Taylor Quinn

www.Harlequin.com

Printed in U.S.A.

ABOUT THE AUTHOR

With fifty-seven original novels, published in more than twenty languages, Tara Taylor Quinn is a *USA TODAY* best-selling author. She is a winner of the 2008 National Readers' Choice Award, four-time finalist for the RWA Rita® Award, a finalist for the Reviewers' Choice Award, the Booksellers' Best Award, the Holt Medallion and appears regularly on Amazon bestsellers lists. Tara Taylor Quinn is a past president of the Romance Writers of America and served for eight years on its board of directors. She is in demand as a public speaker and has appeared on television and radio shows across the country, including *CBS Sunday Morning.* Tara is a spokesperson for the National Domestic Violence Hotline, and she and her husband, Tim, sponsor an annual inline skating race in Phoenix to benefit the fight against domestic violence.

When she's not at home in Arizona with Tim and their canine owners, Jerry Lee and Taylor Marie, or fulfilling speaking engagements, Tara spends her time traveling and inline skating.

Books by Tara Taylor Quinn

Other titles by this author available in ebook format.

For Rachel

CHAPTER ONE

SOMETHING WASN'T RIGHT. Something besides the hot chocolate splashed across the cream-colored silk blouse and brown-linen slacks that twenty-nine-year-old Emma Sanderson had come home to change.

Pulling her key from the lock that Friday morning in early September, she stood just inside the open front door of her two-story townhome, allowing the screen door to close behind her. She listened. But heard nothing.

Was Rob home?

She was in a hurry to get back to the high school before study hall ended and twenty-two fifteen-year-olds converged on her American History class. So she'd parked her car in the driveway and come in by way of the front porch, rather than through the garage as usual.

Was someone in the house? Rob Evert, her fiancé of two years, was attending an accounting seminar at a local college that morning. Besides, the sweet citrusy smell in the air wasn't something she associated with Rob.

With her finger on the pepper-spray tube attached to her key chain, Emma moved forward a couple of steps. She should probably head right back outside. Call the police.

Then she'd be late for class. She had to change.

And what criminal smelled like citrus?

There was no sign of forced entry.

Maybe, in the back of her mind, Emma knew she didn't need law-enforcement protection. Because if she thought she did, she'd be outside and on the phone. Immediately. She wasn't a risk-taker.

But then, she wasn't going to let the past rob her of her present and future, either. Not anymore. Not since the phone calls she'd received over the past month from a Comfort Cove detective, Ramsey Miller.

Miller's news had upended her world. Frank Whittier, the man she'd spent two years adoring and the next twenty-five years hating, was not guilty of abducting her baby sister. All this time she'd blamed him....

Slipping out of her low-heeled pumps because she had to change her pants, Emma crept up the stairs. Someone could be up there.

Probably not. She was overreacting to the citrusy smell.

It was *her* house. She wasn't going to let paranoia run her out of the home she owned, the home shared with her fiancé.

Hugging the fall-foliage wallpaper—everything was fall for Emma, since the fall day Claire had disappeared—she listened as she rose slowly to the second floor.

Definite rustling sounds came from the upper region of her home. As if someone was moving around, but not opening drawers or closets. Or throwing things.

Her mother, who lived nearby, had a key, but Mom wouldn't stop in without asking permission first. And, as the principal of a local school, Rose Sanderson was at work.

The only other person who had a key, besides Emma, was Rob. And he'd lied to her once before about his attendance at a seminar. He'd sworn he'd never lie to her again. She'd believed him enough to let him move in with her.

But she didn't fully trust him.

Her issue. One she was working on.

Their bedroom was the first door on the left. It had its own attached bath. The second bedroom and smaller bath were to the right.

She looked that way first. Surely the intruder wasn't in *her* room.

At the top of the stairs, Emma paused, flicking her long dark curls back over her shoulder, suddenly questioning the wisdom of her actions. The rustling was louder, but steady. A familiar rhythm. Clearly she hadn't been discovered yet.

And then she heard the familiar moan. Short, staccato, deep in the throat. Followed by a longer, louder, expression of relief. The moan she'd thought had been particular to *her*. The one only she could elicit.

He was in their room. For a brief second, as she rounded the corner toward the open door, Emma wondered if he was alone. Hoped he was.

If so, she could slip away, pretend she hadn't seen, and they could continue to...

The woman was on the bottom, her naked backside sinking into the freshly laundered gold sheets Emma had just put on the queen-size bed that morning. Blond hair splayed across Emma's pillow.

"Oh, God."

The other woman was looking at her.

On another day, any day previous to the last phone call from Ramsey Miller, Emma would have turned around and left Rob to get his mess cleaned up and out of their house.

And then, when enough time had passed to take away the sting of his betrayal, she'd have listened patiently while he expressed his self-condemnation and regret. She'd have let him beg. And then she'd have taken him back.

This wasn't the first time he'd been unfaithful to her. But it was the first in their bed. In her home. The first since he'd put the huge diamond ring on her finger.

At least the first she knew of…

Thoughts sped through Emma's mind as she stood frozen and watched the slender long legs disentangle themselves from the man and the sheets.

Rob rolled to his side and Emma pulled the ring off her left hand. He noticed her standing there.

The instant consternation on his face couldn't have been faked. Nor could the sorrow in his eyes.

"Emma, baby, I…"

Ignoring the woman who was in Emma's peripheral vision pulling on sweatpants and a T-shirt, Emma approached the bed and held out the ring to Rob.

"I see she dressed up for the occasion," she

said calmly, as if they were discussing what color to paint the bedroom walls.

"Emma, please…" Rob, looked at her pleadingly, holding the sheet around his naked midsection despite the fact that both women in the room clearly knew what the covered parts looked like. He didn't reach for the ring. But he'd expect it back. He was an accountant. Money mattered.

She placed the two-carat promise on the corner of the dresser. Grabbed a hanger out of the closet that held one of her three-piece suits—the tailored black slacks and jacket and red short-sleeved blouse—grabbed her most expensive black pumps and marched toward the door.

"I'm going back to work," she said, facing the open door, effectively blocking the blond woman's escape. "I'll go straight to Mom's afterward, spend the night there and return here in the morning to meet a locksmith who will be changing the locks." She owned the place. She could do this. "You have until then to clean out anything of yours you want to keep. The furniture all stays. The payments you helped make are in lieu of rent for the past two years."

She heard her voice and wondered at the

woman speaking. She didn't recognize a thing about her. But, damn, her words felt good.

"Emma…"

She heard scrambling behind her, a thump as Rob's feet landed on the floor, and then his footsteps behind her.

"Emma!"

Head high, she just kept walking. Down the stairs. Out the front door. Knowing he couldn't follow her. He hadn't had time to pull on his pants.

In a nearby gas-station bathroom, as she changed her clothes, Emma crumpled, half dressed, on the toilet. She started to cry. To panic. To hurt.

But she didn't go back.

And that afternoon, when she left school, she didn't back down.

THE FUNERAL WAS SO CROWDED that early September Friday afternoon that more than half the attendees had to stand. Forty-year-old Chris Talbot was one of those standing, holding his place in a back corner of the big old Comfort Cove church with shoulders grown thick from a lifetime of lobstering. Fishing was a dangerous business. The most dangerous in the world if you believed what you saw on television.

To Chris it was a way of life. The only way of life.

It had been that way for Wayne Ainge, too, though Chris had barely known the young man whose funeral he'd given up a day of work to attend. Wayne was only twenty. He'd arrived in Comfort Cove from Alaska that summer. Had signed on with one of Chris's competitors. And three days ago he'd gotten his foot tangled up in a trapline and was pulled from his boat to the bottom of the ocean. He'd drowned before anyone could get to him.

The accident had not been the boy's fault. It hadn't been anything he could prevent. A wind had come up, a wave, just as he'd been hoisting a trap overboard, forcing him into one small step to keep his balance. The one small step had cost him his life.

His wasn't the first industry death, by a long shot.

But it was Comfort Cove's first in more than fifty years. The first in Chris's lifetime.

Wayne's father spoke. His brother did, too. A man of the cloth—Chris wasn't a church-going man so he wasn't sure if the man was a priest or pastor or what—read from the Bible and asked them all to pray.

Chris bowed his head out of respect for

Wayne's family, who'd flown in from Alaska to bury their son where he'd said his heart was—the Atlantic Ocean. And then, as people began to file out, he shook hands with his fellow fishermen and their families.

None of them looked one another in the eye.

Every fisherman knew that any one of them could be in that casket up there. It was only by the grace of God that they made it safely home each day.

CHAPTER TWO

"WHAT'S WRONG?" Fifty-six-year-old Rose Sanderson frowned. The expression did nothing to mar her exquisite beauty. Just as all the years of anguish had never done.

As long as Emma didn't look in her mother's eyes. There wasn't a lot of beauty there anymore. Only worry. Angst. Sadness. And pain.

"Sit down, Mom." Emma pulled out one of the metal-rimmed Naugahyde chairs in her mother's kitchen—chairs that matched the metal-rimmed Formica-topped table that had been in that same exact place in the same exact house for the past twenty-five years.

Emma had been able to convince her mother to update the rest of the house over the years. But not that table. It was the last place that Rose had seen her baby girl alive—kneeling on one of those chairs at that table eating her breakfast like a "big people."

Rose wouldn't change that table, and she would never move—no matter how much the neighborhood changed. Rose couldn't leave the only place Claire would know to come back to.

As though she would remember; Claire had been two when she was abducted.

Rose's crystalline blue eyes were wide and worried as Emma sat and folded her hands at the table. "Tell me."

She had to tell her mother about Detective Miller's phone calls. Most particularly the last one.

She'd been deliberating for a couple of days about what she was going to say.

Tonight, with Rob's infidelity a fresh and burning sting, she couldn't seem to find the usual decorum, the caution, with which she couched everything she told her mother.

She didn't recognize herself in the woman who was pushing her to do something more. To be something different.

To change what Rose wouldn't have changed.

"I've spent my entire life playing it safe." They weren't the words she'd come to say.

Rose's frown deepened. "What do you mean?"

"I settle," Emma said. "Or maybe I don't, I don't know." This was her mother. She could only say so much.

Or stray too far from herself...

She was in no state to tell her mother about Ramsey Miller's phone call—about the horrible mistake she and Rose had made, believing all these years that Frank Whittier, her mother's fiancé at the time, had abducted Claire.

"I broke up with Rob today." And that was not a mistake. No matter how badly Rose took the news.

Rose's eyes held a spark of…something… as she watched Emma, saying nothing. But the woman wasn't falling apart so Emma continued.

"I came home and found him with another woman in our bed. I gave him until tomorrow morning to get out."

Rose nodded.

Her mother's expression wasn't crumpling. Or, worse, filling with fear. She almost had a hint of a smile on her face. And she was nodding!

Had the whole world gone mad? Or only Emma's portion of it?

"What? You knew he was seeing someone?"

"Of course not. I'd have told you if I'd known that. I just knew he wasn't right for you."

That almost made her angry. As angry as

she could ever get with the woman who'd suffered so horribly. And tried so hard to love Emma enough. "You thought Rob was wrong for me?"

"Yes." Rose squeezed her hand. "But regardless of what I thought, you loved him and you most definitely didn't deserve to be cheated on. I know it hurts and I'm so sorry about that."

Shaking her head, Emma ignored the compassion in her mother's voice. This was no time to open her heart and give in to the weakness there—a desperate need to be loved, in spite of everything.

She was better off if she kept her walls up.

"Why didn't you say anything?" She concentrated on the facts that perplexed more than they caused pain.

"Because I knew you'd figure it out on your own and that you would be so much stronger for having done so. Acting on my say-so could have crippled you."

"I'd have married him, Mom." If Rob hadn't kept putting off choosing a date. A location. Colors. Anything at all to do with them actually saying "I do," rather than just "I'm going to."

Rose shook her head. "I don't think so."

"But if I had? You'd have let me?"

Rose studied her and then said, "I'm not sure. There was always the chance that I was wrong."

"You liked him. From the first time we met him at that fingerprinting clinic, you liked how he took a real interest in our quest."

"He was a big help. And had good ideas. He was a pleasant conversationalist, but that doesn't mean I thought he'd make you happy. I did like that he kept you here in the area, close by. I liked that he was willing to spend time with us together. That we could do family things."

A given. Rose had lost one daughter. And ever since that day, until Emma had met Rob, it had always been just the two of them.

"I'm not going to leave you, Mom, you know that," Emma said. "Not for anything, or anyone." But for the first time, the words didn't flow from her heart as easily as they flowed past her throat.

For the first time, she wished, just for a second, that she could be as free as other women her age.

And then, ashamed of herself, she gave her mother a hug.

Emma missed Claire like she'd miss an arm or a leg. And she'd only been four when her little sister had been taken. Rose, a single mother who'd lost her baby, had suffered so much more.

Emma's job, as the one left behind, was to be there for Rose. Period.

She wasn't herself right then. Who knew, maybe she wouldn't ever be exactly herself again. But her role in her mother's life would not—could not—change.

"Never say never, Em. You have a life to live," Rose said, sadness mingling with the compassion in her tone. "You have to go where it takes you."

"My place is here. With you."

"I hope it is. But if it's not, you have to go."

Her mother was talking crazy. She wasn't going anywhere.

"You don't mean that. You need me here."

"Yes." Rose's expression was completely sober. "But *my* life doesn't take precedence over yours. Or it shouldn't. And I've begun to see that maybe, in spite of all of my intentions to the contrary, it has."

Emma didn't know what to say. Her mother was right about one thing. She did have a life to live. And she hadn't been living it.

Any other time her mother's words would have frightened her. Tonight, they seemed to make a confusing kind of sense.

CHRIS SKIPPED THE CHURCH meal that followed the funeral, though he did keep his head low—in deference to his mother who would be disappointed in his manners if she were still alive—as he made his way back to the new black Ford truck he'd bought the previous spring.

He wasn't in a hurry to be anywhere. Late-afternoon sunshine usually signaled waiting his turn to meet with Manny, Comfort Cove's lobster dealer, and exchange the day's catch for the current pitiful rate of three dollars per pound. And then there were always things to do on board the *Son Catcher* to occupy his time until dusk—like keeping the aging engine running until the economy recovered enough to shoot lobster prices back up to a price lobstermen could afford to work for.

Today, for the first time in memory, the dock didn't call to him. His first Friday off in months and, while he missed the water, the exertion, the thrill of the catch, the dock was not a happy place that day. They'd lost one of their own.

It could happen.

Wayne Ainge had been far too young to die. By all accounts he'd worshipped the ocean. And she'd been fickle to him.

He might have been driving aimlessly, but

Chris's new truck already seemed to know Chris. Without any conscious decision making, he ended up at Citadel's, an upscale lounge and eatery in the middle of Main Street, the part of the tourist district the city council had sunk all the city's money into.

Fishermen didn't frequent Main Street.

Chris parked in his usual Friday-night spot—albeit a few hours earlier than normal—and, pausing to check out the thronging visitors on both sides of the street he slowly pocketed his keys, went inside and took a seat at the bar.

He was one of two people there. The other, a woman of indiscriminate age, eyed him up and down as though analyzing how much he'd bring per pound.

"Hey, Chris, what's up?" Cody, the bartender, distracted him from a mental rundown of random ways to avoid hookers. "I've never seen you in here before dark."

"Day off work," Chris said, shrugging, and then remembered his attire. He looked just as he always did on Friday nights—like a white-collar business man relaxing after a long week of work. Not like a man from the docks after a long hard day. "Pour me a double," he said.

A good bartender, Cody reached for the

bottle of high-end scotch that Chris favored and poured twice the amount of Chris's preferred drink without saying another word.

Tipping his glass to the younger man, Chris sipped, in memory of a twenty-year-old kid he'd barely known. And to men that he'd known all his life. Fellow lobstermen, fishermen, who risked their lives every day earning a living in spite of the vagaries of an ocean that was more powerful than all of them.

And halfway through the glass of amber liquid, he drank to her, too. To the mighty Atlantic. The ocean. The reason he would never have a woman in his life.

CHAPTER THREE

"I HAD A CALL, MOM." Emma was helping her mother make a chicken Caesar salad she didn't want. Because it was her and Rose's favorite meal. A feel-good meal. Security food.

"From who?"

She had to start living her own life—and she wasn't even sure what that meant. To date, her life consisted of responsibilities and "shoulds" and protecting Rose. She had to be free from some of that—free to take a chance or two. To be spontaneous in spite of dangers.

Free to want.

Rob had been naked in their bed, her bed—on sheets she'd purchased and laundered—with another woman.

Because Emma was so lacking? She'd never had an orgasm. Was that her fault? Or his?

"Emma?"

Rose's brow was wrinkled as she glanced her way. "What?" Thank God Rose couldn't read her thoughts.

"You said you'd had a call. I asked who from."

Back on track. Not that the coming conversation was going to be any easier than the silent one she'd been having on and off with herself since noon that day. "From a detective. Here in Comfort Cove. His name's Ramsey Miller." None of which mattered. *Get to the point.*

Was she not woman enough to hold on to a man? Not adventurous enough? Not wild enough?

Rose wasn't moving. Her hands, holding part of a roasted chicken breast and a knife, were suspended in midair. Midcut. "Tell me." When she finally spoke, her tone was biting.

Emma knew she shouldn't have started this. Not tonight. There was no reason to put her mother through more days and weeks of anguish while hope battled with reality. Reality always won. They knew that.

And yet, she really should tell Rose about Miller's call. At some point, the detective might need to speak with her mother.

"No one knows anything about Claire," she said quickly.

At the sink, she turned on the cold water to rinse the lettuce.

"What, then?" Fear entered Rose's tone.

Emma had known it would. That happened to a woman when her baby was stolen out of her home in broad daylight.

She thought about the box of forensic evidence that had gone missing from the police station. It was the reason for Miller's initial call more than a month before. The last time Emma had seen the box containing her and Cal's and Claire's belongings, she'd been four years old.

Miller had no idea who'd taken the evidence or why.

But Rose would draw her own conclusions. And she would inevitably get her hopes up. Emma knew how it worked. Not just because she'd lived close to her mother all these years, but because she lived with the same ups and downs.

If someone had stolen the evidence from her sister's case, could it mean that Claire was still alive? Still out there?

Or, conversely, did it mean that her baby sister was dead and buried and her abductor wanted to make certain she stayed that way?

"Emma, you're scaring me." Her mother still held the chicken and the knife.

Emma had moved on to mixing the oil and spices for the dressing, putting them together just the way they liked. Soft scents from the loaf of fresh Italian bread warming in the oven wafted around them.

She wasn't up to this conversation. As a good daughter, she had to let her mother know what was going on because she couldn't guarantee that Frank wouldn't call. She didn't think he would. But he knew where Rose lived. He could send her a letter.

Emma didn't want to sit and eat. Didn't want to do what she always did. She wanted to go somewhere. Do something.

She wanted to escape. From Rose. Claire's memory. Frank and Cal Whittier. Rob.

She was twenty-nine. If she didn't start living life now, it could all be over before it even began.

Taking the knife and chicken from her mother's lifeless hands, Emma started to cut.

"Cal Whittier wrote a book."

"What?" Rose's brows drew together and she sank down into the chair at the head of the table—ironically, the one that had been Frank's during the time he and his son, Cal, had lived with them.

Back when they'd been a real family.

"He published a book?" Rose asked.

"No." Dropping the knife in the sink, Emma left the salad and went to sit next to her mother. "He gave it to Detective Miller, who works cold cases. Miller read it and noticed a piece of information that Cal had put down that wasn't in any of the recorded testimony."

"What information?" Rose's tone was suspicious. Did she think Cal would lie? He'd only been seven when Claire had gone missing.

Although Emma had only been four at the time, she could still remember the anguish in her almost-brother's eyes when he realized that, because of him, the police thought his father had done something to Claire.

"Do you remember that meat delivery truck that used to come here?" Emma asked. She'd remembered it, as she'd told Detective Miller when he'd asked her.

"Of course. They stopped three doors down, every Wednesday morning. Delivered to the Bryants. Why?"

"Cal mentioned the truck in his book. He hid behind it the morning that...that morning when he left for school. He sneaked from there to hide behind another car and then made a dash for the backyard so he didn't have to go to school."

"He'd thrown up in gym the day before," Rose said, her tone softer. "He was so embarrassed he begged us to let him stay home. We hated to make him go, but we knew that if we didn't the problem would only escalate."

"Like falling off a horse," Emma said, the words coming to her from long ago. "I remember Frank telling Cal about falling off a horse and getting right back on."

"I remember that." Emma couldn't see Rose's expression. Her mother's head was bent.

"Apparently Cal didn't tell the police that part back then," Emma said, choosing her words carefully so her mother wouldn't get her hopes up. "When Detective Miller read about the truck, he remembered another unsolved abduction where there'd been mention of a delivery truck, so he followed up on it."

Rose's head shot up, her gaze stark. "He found something? Did…is Claire…"

Shaking her head, Emma squeezed her mother's hand. "No, Mom. I told you. There's been no word of Claire."

"But there might be. That's what you're telling me? They have a lead?"

"No," Emma said emphatically. "It turned out that the other abduction Detective Ramsey remembered reading about was unrelated. Since then he's found two other abductions in Massachusetts that both took place more than ten years ago, on delivery routes, but they haven't turned up any connection to us. Or her."

Swallowing against the tightness in her throat, Emma plowed on. "Detective Miller found the driver of our truck, though. He talked to him, and—"

"He knew something? What did he say? What does he—"

"Mom, please. This is why I didn't want to tell you."

"Emma, for God's sake, she was my daughter. I'm never going to stop caring, or hurting, and so I react strongly, but that's no reason not to tell me.…"

Emma could have reminded her mother about the times Rose had shut herself away for days, the times her mother had cried for so many hours on end that Emma'd had to fend for herself, about the times she'd had to beg her mother to eat so Rose would have the energy to get out of bed.

"The driver saw Claire in the front yard, Mom. He passed Cal going up the street and he said it looked like Claire was watching him. It bothered him to see such a young child outside alone so he drove by again after making his delivery. That's when he saw Frank come out of the house with his briefcase, which he put into the empty backseat of the car, and then he got in the car alone and drove away. That was six minutes *after* he'd seen Claire in the yard alone. And based on the timing, it would've been *after* Cal had seen Claire in Frank's car."

Rose's eyes looked sunken and her mouth hung open as she stared at Emma, at Emma's lips, as though trying to decipher the words that had just passed through them.

"What are you saying? That Frank didn't do it?" The words were a whisper, more movement than sound.

Shaking her head, Emma held on to the woman who'd raised her well, in spite of her heartbreak. "The driver's testimony matched Frank's testimony from twenty-five years ago word for word. He's been exonerated."

Rose's eyes raised to meet Emma's gaze. "Frank didn't do it."

"No, Mom."

"I can't…we…he was persecuted…"

And when investigators had failed to turn up enough proof to charge Frank with the crime for which he'd been arrested, he'd been run out of town like a low-life criminal, Emma silently filled in the blank Rose's words left hanging.

And worse, they'd kept tabs on him, contacted school officials who might hire the ex-principal and coach, preventing Frank from getting a job in the field he loved so he wouldn't harm another child. Rose and Emma had spoken openly at conference after conference, educating the public about child-safety issues, raising money for the search for missing children and talking about the man who still walked free.…

They hadn't named Frank. That would have been illegal. But they'd introduced themselves. They'd talked about Claire by name. And anyone who'd wanted to know more could have found out anything they wanted. Including Frank's name.

Frank and Cal had been kicked out of town—but first, they'd been kicked out of the family.

Rose processed the news silently. Emma's heart cried for both of them.

She breathed a sigh of relief when her mother finally spoke. "Have you heard from him?"

"No. I really don't think they'd contact us, Mom. Not after…"

Beside herself with grief the day Claire had disappeared, Rose had latched on to any hope at all of finding Claire—even if that meant she believed her fiancé was the one who could lead them to Claire. She'd latched on and lashed out. With a vengeance.

"I… Oh, my God…"

"Detective Miller told me they're living in Tyler, Tennessee," Emma said slowly. "They know your address. I'd be shocked if we heard from them…but we might. So…"

"They? They…who?"

"Cal and Frank."

Rose didn't ask the question Emma read in her mother's eyes. "Neither of them ever married. They still share a home. Cal's an English professor at Tyler University, Mom."

"A professor?" Rose's lips tilted slightly upward.

Emma smiled. "Yeah." She'd missed him so much over the years. They'd only lived together a year, but there'd been no doubt in Emma's mind that Cal was her big brother.

That he'd always be there to look out for her. Protect her.

Minutes passed. "And Frank?"

"He worked as a janitor until just recently."

"A janitor?"

"In a nursing home."

"I have to call Cal, Mom." Emma finally got to the real point of the conversation. "I can't not call him." And she couldn't contact Rose's ex-fiancé's son without letting her mother know.

"I accused an innocent man...." Rose's words trailed off and hung there.

"You were a mother who had to do whatever she could to find her missing child."

"I threw him out. Threw them out..."

"You were agonized."

"I sent letters, contacted schools...."

"You did what you felt you had to do to protect other children." The crusade to stop Frank Whittier had probably saved Rose's life. It had certainly given Emma her mother back, as it had provided Rose with an outlet for her anguish.

"You did what any mother would have done, given the evidence." From his backyard hideout, Cal had seen Claire in his father's car. When the police had searched the car, they'd found Claire's favorite teddy bear, the one she'd slept with the night before and brought to breakfast the morning of her disappearance, under the front seat of Frank Whittier's car.

"Cal was hiding under those bushes that used to be in the backyard. When he first got there, he peeked around the corner to make sure Frank's car was still there. That's when he saw Claire. He didn't look again, but he heard the car drive off. There's no way he or any of us could've known she'd gotten out of the car during those six or so minutes."

Rose's eyes were filled with tears as she looked over at Emma. "I loved him. I should at least have given him the benefit of the doubt."

"At the risk of losing Claire forever?" If Frank had been guilty, and Rose had protected him, stood by him, it could have been too late.

"We did lose her," Rose said. "And we lost Frank and Cal, too."

And Emma and Rose owed the Whittiers the respect of an apology, at the very least.

"I have to call him, Mom." She'd handle this one.

Her mother had forbidden Emma to write to Cal over the years, but she'd wanted to. So badly.

Would her life have been different if she had? Would she have avoided coming home to find another woman in her man's arms if she'd ever, even once, dared to take a chance? To demand for herself as much as she gave to Rose and Claire?

Looking sick to her stomach, Rose nodded, and retreated to the balcony that looked over the Atlantic Ocean, in the distance.

Putting their untouched dinner in the refrigerator, Emma cleaned up and let herself out.

Life wasn't easy. Not for Rose. Not for any of them.

Rose couldn't make things right for her daughters.

Claire was gone.

And Emma just felt dead.

CHAPTER FOUR

THE NUMBER OF TIMES Chris had felt grief were so few and far between he could remember all of them. He relived each and every one as he sat at Citadel's that Friday night and nursed a second glass of not-cheap whiskey. A single shot this time.

Every hurt, every disappointment, every little insecurity he'd ever felt, came back to him as he sat there alone, trying to hold on to faculties he refused to do without.

There was the time his father had called home and asked him to bring his mother to the phone, and Chris, running into her room to get her, had found her beneath a naked man he'd never met in the bed that his parents shared.

He touched briefly on the night Sara had given him back the diamond engagement ring she'd accepted several months before, but didn't allow himself to linger. The void that Sara's leaving him had created was soon filled again—by Sara. She was another man's wife now, but she was Chris's best friend.

He thought about calling her, telling her about Ainge, and took another sip of Scotch instead. Part of the reason she'd left him was because she couldn't live with the constant possibility of his death on the ocean. He didn't need to bring the possibility any closer to home.

Which left Chris with his morose trip down memory lane.

There was the morning he'd received the call that his parents had been killed in a pileup on the freeway just fifteen minutes from home. That was also when he found out they'd been on their way home from a court hearing because his mother, who'd already broken his father's heart, had filed for divorce.

The last time had come a couple of days ago, when word had spread that Wayne Ainge had gone overboard, when they'd all waited as rescue crews attempted to get the young man up from the bottom of the ocean in time to save his life, and then heard the news that they'd failed, that the boy was dead.

Oh, and there was Christmas Day. He always had invitations for the day, places he was wanted and welcome. But for some reason that day got to him. Which was why he was usually the lone boat out on the ocean on December 25.

Still, only a handful of sad memories in forty years... He was a lucky guy.

"You playing tonight?" Cody was back, tipping the bottle over the top of Chris's glass. He might have stopped him. Probably should have. Instead, he allowed the younger man to fill his glass and then raised it to his waiting lips.

The piano up on the dais was the reason he was there.

"Yeah," he answered after he sipped.

Nodding, Cody headed down the bar. Chris was pretty sure he heard him say "Good," but he could have just imagined it. No matter. He didn't play for Cody. Or for anyone.

He played because music was good for the soul.

And because he could.

He played because doing so helped ease the tension that came with lobstering every day of your life.

SHE'D GIVEN ROB twenty-four hours to get out of the house. She'd told him she was going to stay with her mother. She'd known she could. Truthfully, she hadn't planned anything. Contrary to her normal way, she'd spoken without first analyzing the various ramifications of her decision.

She didn't have a house to go home to. She'd left her mother's and she wasn't going back that night.

Her attachment to her mother was probably part of the reason Rob had cheated on her. A woman with her mother attached to her hip couldn't be much of a turn-on.

A woman who couldn't climax probably wasn't much of a turn-on, either. Lord knew she tried, but her body didn't seem to be capable of letting go.

And even if her relationship with Rose had nothing to do with any of her problems, Emma needed to be away from her mother long enough to be able to breathe on her own.

First, she needed a place to spend the night.

She'd walked out without packing so much as a toothbrush.

She kept one at her mom's. Along with pajamas and changes of clothes. Maybe she should go back. It made sense to go back. What was one more night going to hurt?

She could start her new life tomorrow. Right after she changed the locks on her doors.

And what if Rob was at her townhome

tomorrow, waiting for her? What if he tried to change her mind? There she'd be, going straight from her mother's house back to the secure life Rob offered her—albeit a life spent putting up with Rob's philandering ways.

No, she couldn't go to her mother's. She couldn't show up at home tomorrow, the same woman she was today—the woman who hadn't been exciting enough to hold her man's interest.

She couldn't go home as the woman who settled for safety and security.

If she was going to change her life, it had to be tonight. She had to take a chance. To do something, anything, that wasn't her norm. She had to be someone different.

Switching from her MP3 player, which was loaded with classics—soft and soothing music that was there to relax her after a day with rambunctious high schoolers—Emma stopped at the first satellite radio station that was blaring a beat.

The LED dash display broadcast the song title and artist in little green letters. She recognized neither and turned up the volume. She'd drown out her thoughts. And if she ever found a song she knew, she'd scream the words at the top of her lungs and pretend that she was singing along.

THREE HOURS INTO Friday evening, Chris was on his third drink. He wasn't drunk, but even the ageless hag at the bar was beginning to look a little better.

Awaiting his turn on the piano, he listened to his competitors pounding the keys of the baby grand on the raised carpeted dais that was the restaurant's centerpiece. The dais turned; the tables surrounding it did not.

The gleaming black instrument shone under professional spotlights and was the only furniture on the stage.

Chris's number in the single elimination competition was up soon. He'd won the last draw of the night, which meant that he'd be up against the pianist voted by preselected judges as the best of the bunch. Chris liked the spot because he could stay onstage after he'd finished his set and play for as many hours as it took to wipe away the tension from the past week.

He didn't need another win. He needed relaxation. He needed peace.

He needed to forget the grieving faces of those who'd loved—and lost—a man of the sea.

THE PLACE SMELLED as heavenly as she'd remembered—a mixture of spices, freshly baked rolls and prime cuts of steak marinated in Citadel's secret sauce. Locals didn't usually patronize the glitzy establishments on the tourist strip in downtown Comfort Cove, but a son of one of the teachers at school had played in a piano competition there a couple of times and Emma had accompanied the divorced mother on both occasions.

Now, sitting alone at the bar—something she'd never have considered doing before—she sipped a glass of white wine and concentrated on convincing herself that she could stay right where she was at least until she finished her drink.

Making deals with herself.

If she stayed fifteen minutes, she could make a trip to the ladies' room to reassess.

If she stayed half an hour, she could think about getting a table. Maybe even order something to eat. If she made it an hour, she'd have to call someone—her divorced teacher friend, probably—and let her know where she was.

If she had more than two glasses of wine she'd call a cab....

To take her...where?

Raising the heavy crystal glass to her lips,

she gulped. She'd figure that out later. There were plenty of hotels downtown.

And because she paid her credit card off every single month, she had plenty of limit to cover whatever exorbitant fee they'd charge.

She'd show Rob....

No. She was there to show herself something. To save her life.

She sipped again, raised her gaze and took in the people around her. A couple of men sitting alone at the bar, both dressed in suits with their ties loosened at the collar. A woman who was also alone and probably there on business. Just not the white-collar kind.

There were couples—both at the bar and filling the tables around the center stage—but those she ignored. And there were families, healthy groups of people who laughed and talked and fought and took one another for granted. She'd spent a lot of her youth wondering what it felt like to be one of them.

And then she'd grown up and realized she could make a family of her own. That's where Rob had come in. They had plans to make a family.

And she'd kicked him out.

She had to phone him. To apologize for

her hastiness. He'd be expecting the call. So maybe she should text him instead.

"And I did it my..." She suddenly heard the famous melody and it caught her attention.

Reaching beneath her jacket to make sure that her red silk blouse was still tucked into her black slacks, Emma sat up straighter. The words continued to play in her mind.

But they'd been placed there by the pianist up onstage. The timing seemed odd. Fortuitous. As though this song had been chosen for *her*. A song about facing the end of one's life with absolutely no regrets.

And the way to do that?

Live by the dictates of your own heart. And only your heart.

Have I ever done that?

Emma sipped her wine.

She watched the pianist's strong masculine fingers fly over the keys. She'd seen him play before. He'd won the competition on both the nights she'd been there.

Forgoing her fifteen-minute-mark trip to the ladies' room, she ordered a second glass of wine and let the music envelop her. The man played with more passion than Emma had ever dared feel in her entire life.

And he did so as though completely unaware of all of the people watching him from the tables below.

If there'd been a competition that evening, it was over.

The man with the weathered face and long-ish hair had the stage all to himself.

HE'D WON AGAIN. If Chris were the sort to care about what other people thought, he'd probably be embarrassed. He didn't care. So he wasn't.

He also wasn't stone-cold sober, not that anyone was paying his state of inebriation any mind. His room at the inn across the street would be waiting for him. He rarely used it, but every Friday night he had a free room at his disposal—paid for by Citadel's owner as part of their business agreement.

Tonight he was going to use that room.

Breaking into one of his own compositions, a piece that flew from his fingers without any conscious thought, he let the music take him on his own private journey. He was a little boy, scared of the waves that crashed against his father's boat. And he was the waves, with the strength and the will to steal men from their lives, their loved ones. He was the source of all power. Others were afraid; he was invigorated.

He played until he trembled from the inside out, until emotion rose in his chest, and threatened to choke him. And still he played.

With the demons of hell at his back, with the determination to go to his own grave with no regrets, he ran as fast and as far as he could from the sight of a mother's face who'd buried her son that day, from the memories of the faces of the other women there—those who, except for a fate he'd never understand, could have been the ones grieving. He ran from the expressions on the faces of the men left behind who would not—could not—spare their loved ones the risk of a similar fate.

And maybe, just maybe, he ran from the fact that he was all alone.

EMMA WASN'T PARTICULARLY hungry. But she ordered food, anyway, so that she had an excuse to stay in her seat at the bar and continue to lose herself in the music emanating from the fingers of a man she'd never met but knew she'd never forget.

He'd changed her life that night. He'd shared his music with her, wrapped her in its graces, holding her there so that she didn't run back home.

She ordered more wine, too. A third glass.

The pianist pulled things from her raw and gaping heart that were unfamiliar to her. Parts of herself she hadn't had to face. He held her fast in life's grip, keeping her rooted in that seat.

She ate a little bit. Pushed the plate away and sipped her wine and listened. It was after midnight. The man had been playing, with only one small break, for more than two hours.

He was bound to stop soon.

She couldn't bear the thought. Not now. Not yet. She wasn't ready for him to let her go, to leave her to fend for herself.

She wasn't changed enough.

She needed more.

She had to meet him.

CHAPTER FIVE

WITH HANDS USED to pulling in heavy lobster traps in rapid succession, Chris communed with the ivories. The music his playing sent out into the night was a byproduct—he felt melodies and harmonies and chords more than he heard them. He didn't understand how it worked—the music and his inner self healing. He didn't ask. He just presented himself to the keys and played until he knew he was done.

Until he knew he could sleep.

At least, that was how it had always worked before.

So why wasn't it working?

When midnight passed and he was still driven to play, when the tunes he produced changed from popular ditties to intense renditions of classical masterpieces with a few of his own compositions mixed in, when his fingertips grew numb with pounding, he ordered a fourth drink to help the peace he was seeking find him more easily. To assist the piano in its work.

"You're here late tonight," Cody said as he delivered the drink himself. Other than a waitress on the floor and the checker at the door, Cody was the only employee left for the night. The kitchen had been closed for a couple of hours.

"So are you," Chris said, tipping his glass to the friendly guy. "I'll bet your wife has a bit to say about that." About the long hours. The time away.

"As long as I get home in time to crawl into bed with her, she doesn't complain," Cody said. "I'm home with her and the kids during the day and now that they're in preschool we've got lots of time just the two of us. It's nice."

Chris nodded, one hand on the keys, trying to imagine what it would be like to be home with a wife and kids even for an hour, and coming up blank.

"Who's the woman?" He'd noticed the woman in the tailored black suit and red silky-looking top over the past few hours and she was something he could converse about, though why he had a sudden urge to hang out with the bartender was a mystery.

"Not sure," Cody said. "I don't know her and she hasn't said much."

She'd had plenty of male admirers. Chris would guess just about every adult male in the place had given her the once-over. More than once.

"Someone probably stood her up," he said, taking another sip. The liquor was warm going down. Felt good. "Can't imagine why, though. She's a looker." In a nonarty sort of way. Long legged, and even in the conservative black slacks and jacket her curves caught his attention.

The woman didn't need jewelry or makeup to call attention to herself. Hell, he'd bet she'd look good in an old robe and shower cap.

But what a shame it would be to hide that head of hair. He couldn't seem to push away the image of those long dark curls splayed across a rumpled white pillowcase. He sipped again, enjoying the mental image for another second.

"She's sure been looking at you, man," Cody said, turning to eye the woman, who was holding her almost-empty wineglass by the stem with both hands.

Chris had noticed. He'd made eye contact a time or two. Had nodded and received a nod in return.

"She been talking to anybody?"

"Nope."

"No one?"

"Nope."

"Not even on a cell phone?"

"Nope. No texting, either."

"An out-of-towner?"

"Here on business? Knows no one? Most likely," Cody said.

She glanced their way. Held up her glass with a smile that was more shy than flirtatious.

Chris tapped a chord. And taking one more sip of whiskey, he started to play again.

SHE WAS THE sixth-to-the-last patron in the bar. Two separate tables, a couple at each, were still occupied. And the leathery-skinned woman who still sat at the other end of the bar. The woman talked to pretty much anyone who sat near her, but so far she was alone.

Maybe she wasn't a working girl as she'd first assumed. Maybe she was the wife or girlfriend of the piano player? Used to sitting by herself all night while her man worked?

Keeping watch over him?

Like she should have kept watch over Rob?

One o'clock in the morning and Emma still had no place to be. Or desire to go.

She couldn't drive anywhere. That decision had been made with her last glass of wine.

One of the hotels on the block was going to be her accommodation. Didn't matter which one. They were all nice. All clean. In a safe area. And, because it was fall and not summer, they'd be sure to have rooms available.

Piano man glanced at her. Again. Emma should have looked away. Any other time she would have.

His glance called to her. She heard him. Those eyes said he found her interesting. She told him his music moved her.

He felt her pain. She was aware of his depths.

They were two intense people meeting on a level that no one else could share.

Or at least that's how she translated their silent communications.

She'd never been intense before. Never even gave herself a chance to see if she could be.

She was different tonight. Allowing herself to just be. Watching, as if from afar, to see who might emerge. Maybe, just maybe, she was finding the person inside of her that she'd kept locked up tight since the day Claire went missing.

And even if this woman was only allowed

out of her cage for this one night, Emma was determined to give her life.

So she sipped her wine. And she participated in nonverbal conversations.

She'd go get her hotel room. As soon as piano man was done for the night. As long as he was going to play for her, she was going to stay and listen.

CODY WOULDN'T TELL him to leave. Don Carmine, Cody's boss and owner of Citadel's, would have his hide if the bartender in any way offended the provider of Citadel's discounted lobster supply. One of the best deals Chris had ever made—his lobster in exchange for 24/7 use of the baby grand, accomodations across the street when he wanted them, and whatever he wanted to drink. Chris didn't abuse those privileges.

He didn't usually stay late, either, but tonight he couldn't bring himself to leave. Not while the long-legged woman still sat at the bar watching him.

His mystery woman played him just right. She made no demands or requests. Nothing he'd have to reject. She was just there. And she was exquisite.

Chris softened his touch on the keys, caressing them, telling the woman through his playing that she moved him.

He found it curious that she didn't seem to have much awareness of her effect on other people. He hadn't seen her so much as make eye contact with a single one of the men who'd been buzzing around her that night.

A woman alone keeping to herself wasn't so unusual—what struck him was the way her shoulders pulled in slightly instead of squaring off, her air of hesitation, the fact that every time he caught her eye, she always glanced away first.

A glass appeared on the cork-lined black tray sitting on top of the piano, within hands' reach, as he played. A set of keys followed.

"Lock up when you're through." Cody's words could be heard over the ballad Chris was playing.

He glanced around. The place was empty. The waitress—Beth—and the bouncer at the door must've gone home.

His gaze landed back on the woman who was the last remaining customer at the bar.

"She asked if she could stay. I told her it was fine with me as long as it was all right with you."

Watching the woman, who was watching

him, Chris nodded. And as he heard the back door click behind Cody, he started another song.

SHE COULDN'T SPEND the night in a bar. But what difference would it make if Emma checked into a room, with nothing but her purse, at one-thirty in the morning or three-thirty?

Piano man—*Chris,* Cody had told her when he'd poured her last glass of wine, on the house—continued to play. But he watched her, not the keys beneath his fingertips.

That was fine. She was watching him, too.

She wondered about Chris's shoulders, so broad they stretched the long-sleeved white dress shirt he wore. Wondered if playing piano was what he did for a living.

She could have asked Cody.

She hadn't.

Chris raised an eyebrow to her. She tilted her head.

Her breasts felt twice their size as she sat there, staring at him. Her nipples tingled. She had been freed for the night by wine. And music.

She was dangerous.

In that moment Emma liked the change.

As much as she didn't want Chris to stop

playing, she wanted him to stop even more. He had to at some point.

And when he did, what then?

Would he speak to her?

Or simply motion for her to leave so he could lock up and disappear into the night?

Lifting a hand from the piano keys, continuing his auditory art with one-handed playing, he raised his glass to his lips. Sipped slowly. Her fingers shook on the stem of her wineglass as she also lifted her glass, and folded her lips around the rim.

He put down his glass, and she listened for the message the keys would send out as he returned his hand to them. Soft? Sweet? Intense? Deep, dark chords?

But his right hand didn't return to the piano. He held it palm up, and folded three of his strong fingers inward. The fourth, his index finger, he crooked, calling to her.

The new Emma, the one who was refusing to go home to her mother's house, stood. She maintained eye contact. And with desire spiraling in private places, she started toward the piano man with no thoughts of turning back.

CHAPTER SIX

CHRIS HAD NO REAL idea what he was doing. It was late. He had to be on the docks before sunrise—a few short hours away. He'd already missed a day's catch and couldn't afford to miss another.

He started to play another song, his fingers moving naturally over the keys, sending a harmonic rendition of "Send in the Clowns" out into the deserted room. With most of the lights off, he could only make out the first circle of tables around the dais. The rest of the space was black.

Except where the track lighting from the bar—lights that were always left on—accentuated the softly sculpted features of the goddess slowly approaching him.

He switched chords and without pause started in on "Seduces Me"—a song written by Dan Hill and made famous by Céline Dion. He'd heard it many times but had never played it before.

The deceptively simple, sexy melody filled

the air around them, sending shivers down his spine. The woman faltered a step, but didn't look away. Neither did he.

When she reached the dais, his gaze landed for an instant on the vee between her thighs, and then immediately rose to meet the questioning but undeniably sultry look in her eye.

His hands slowed and then stilled completely. He moved sideways on the shiny black bench, watching her, waiting to see what she would do. He wasn't completely sober. He should have stood. Thanked her for her patronage and secured his exit.

But he couldn't. More important than sleep, more important even than the catch, was knowing what she would do next.

EMMA TRIED TO think. She stood outside of her body—a spirit in the air above that dais—and she saw someone with a body who looked like hers, wearing her clothes, standing alone with a man she'd never met.

He'd moved over. And was waiting for her.

He was older than she'd first thought—in his late thirties or early forties. His skin was as leathery as the woman's from the bar earlier that evening. His hands were well worn, too. Rougher than she'd expected for a man who played the piano so beautifully. The dichotomy spoke to her.

Chris was not just a pianist. Emma was not just a safe bet.

She sat down.

HER BODY WAS warm. Chris's body buzzed with anticipation.

"What's your name?" He'd been making eye contact with her all night. Now he looked down at the keys in front of him.

"Emma."

Her hands appeared on the keys, as well. She had slender fingers. Unadorned, although there was a white band against the tanned skin of her left ring finger.

"I'm Chris."

"I know."

He glanced at her. She turned her head. Their gazes were only inches apart now.

"Cody told me," she explained.

"You hungry?"

She licked her lips. "Not really."

"Your glass is almost empty, you want more?"

"Okay."

"The bars are all closed, but I have a room. It's across the street."

He didn't promise to be a gentleman.

"Okay." Her tongue flicked across her bottom lip. His body thrummed his response.

"You want to join me there?"

He would never, ever force himself on a woman, but he wasn't about to turn down any opportunities this beauty—Emma—was willing to offer.

"I think I do."

He had a condom in his wallet. She'd recently had a ring on her finger. Safe enough for him.

"Good," he said, and lowering the lid to protect the piano keys, he rose, took her hand and led them out the back door.

EMMA WASN'T STUPID. She knew what she was agreeing to by leaving the bar with Chris. She just couldn't seem to make herself care.

Because she was numb? Hurt beyond good judgment?

Because she was drunk?

Or because the piano man made her body sing in places a tune had never played?

The warm night air didn't sober her. Or instill her with any better sense. It caressed her skin, heightening the surreal sense of vibrancy she felt as they walked hand in hand across a quiet street lit with old-fashioned gas lamps.

They reached the other side.

"I don't…"

"Don't what?" They were the first words he'd said since he'd locked the door of Citadel's behind them.

Who was she kidding? This was no love tryst. She didn't know anything about the man, except that he'd been endowed with a magnificent talent.

"I reserve the right to change my mind." Emma strove to save herself from the unleashed woman inside of her.

"Of course."

They stopped on the curb in front of one of the more expensive hotels in the tourist district. The doorman stood alert, in spite of the very early morning hour, appearing eager to be of service to them.

Chris's eyes were blue. A vivid, bright blue—not the darker hue they'd appeared to be in the shadows of the restaurant. His hair, falling across his forehead, was dark enough to be almost black.

"You want me to walk you to your car?" he asked. His eyes belied the indifference in his voice.

"No!" She was surprised by the vehemence with which she said it. "I just want… I've heard stories…."

Words escaped her and she waited for him to get her drift.

He was silent.

"It's only fair that you know, going in, that I might change my mind. At an inopportune moment."

He raised one of his strong, gifted hands to her face and ran his fingers through her hair.

"I will stop," he said, looking her straight in the eye. "If at any time, *any time,* you change your mind, I *will* stop."

She believed him. And hoped, God help her, that she wouldn't want him to.

EMMA ALMOST GIGGLED as the elevator opened for them upon approach, as though it had been commanded to do so. Surely Chris didn't have that much power.

Though, judging by the way he made her feel, she couldn't be sure.

"Not many people going up and down at this late hour," he said, stepping inside the car.

"I think I've had a lot to drink," she said, grinning at him.

"Four glasses of wine by my count."

He was counting? She stared at him. He'd been watching her that closely?

"From the moment you walked in tonight, I didn't notice anything else."

It was a good line and she was inebriated enough to like it.

"I'm not kidding," Chris said, his voice deep, a bit husky, reminding her of a well-aged wine. One out of her price league. "I don't play games with women."

"I don't play at all," Emma said, her voice sounding tiny in the confines of the elevator. "This is the first time I've ever done anything like this."

A mood-killer if ever there was one. Yes, she'd discovered new things about herself tonight. But she was still Emma and now she was going to blow this whole thing.

If she did, chances were old Emma would win and she'd have to resign herself to a life of safety and security and settling for Robs.

She nearly laughed out loud at that last thought. *Robs.* Funny word.

But if she succeeded—if she made love with her piano man—she'd be forever changed. She'd no longer be the woman who'd never taken a chance, never faced danger, never had the nerve to do exactly what she felt like doing.

The elevator door slid open and Emma half

expected Chris to gracefully bow out of his invitation.

Holding the door open with his body, he lifted her hand until her gaze followed.

"I'm glad you don't make a habit of this," he said, the smile in his eyes sending her spiraling as though he'd tipped her over the edge of a cliff. "You want to continue?"

"Yes."

He guided her through the door, following closely, and when he came up beside her, he wrapped his arm around her waist.

They faced the elegantly appointed room together. And she tingled with anticipation. Not fear.

In that moment, Emma knew that if the night killed her, she'd die having lived.

And she'd prefer that to living her whole life as if she were already dead.

CHAPTER SEVEN

IT WASN'T SUPPOSED to happen this way.

The words repeated themselves in his mind. He wasn't sure what they meant. But he heard them.

He probably even believed them. There just wasn't a damn thing he could—or wanted to—do about them.

"I have a dry white or merlot," he said as he peered into the stocked refrigerator in the living-room section of his hotel room.

The king-size bed was there, too, in plain view, about ten feet of plush beige carpet away.

Emma sat—still fully dressed down to the low-heeled shoes she wore—on the couch, but based on the stiffness of her posture and the way her gaze kept darting to the oversize armchair next to the couch he had the distinct impression that she'd have been more comfortable in the seat made for one.

He quirked his brow at her. "You ready to say stop?"

"Dry white, please." Her brown gaze swung to him, and stayed there. Steady and strong.

"I'm glad." Really glad. Abnormally glad—Chris had never been hard up for women.

He opened the small bottle, emptied it into one of two wineglasses on the bar, opened a miniature bottle of Crown for himself and poured it into a highball.

Handing her the glass of wine, he took a sip of his whiskey and sat down beside her.

The night might be late, but he felt like they had all the time in the world. And if they didn't, he was going to take it, anyway. This woman, this experience, was not to be rushed.

"You want to know anything more about me?" he asked.

"Yes, but not right now."

Fair enough.

She didn't offer him the same privilege. She pushed her hair back away from her face and he saw that white band on her finger again. She'd said she'd never done anything like this before.

"I'm okay if tonight is a rebound for you. But I need to know that you aren't married. I don't take what belongs to someone else."

"I'm not married."

He felt like grinning. And it wasn't supposed to happen that way, either.

"Have you ever been married?"

"No." She glanced away, as though ashamed.

Chris lifted her hand that held the wineglass and brought it to her lips. "Sip," he said softly. "I haven't ever been married, either." *Almost* didn't count.

His words brought her gaze back to him. "How old are you?" he asked.

She was of age; he knew that. But he was curious.

"Twenty-nine."

Younger than he'd expected. Younger than Sara by eleven years.

"I'm forty."

She had a right to know.

"Okay."

"That doesn't bother you?"

"That you're eleven years older than me?"

His age had never been an issue for him before. He simply hadn't cared to measure life in terms of time. He sipped his drink.

"It doesn't bother me in the least," she said, a small smile forming on the lips that had been calling to him all night long. "As a matter of fact, I find forty kind of sexy. You aren't a kid all filled up with his own sense of importance."

"I could be an older guy all filled up with my own sense of importance."

"You could be." She took a sip of her wine, still smiling. "But I know that you aren't."

"How do you know?"

"You've asked for my permission every step of the way," she said simply. "If you thought you were life's greatest gift, you'd be sure you knew what I wanted—which, by the way would be only what you wanted—and you'd have charged forward with the strength of a bull to get it."

"Apparently you know someone who's filled with his own sense of importance."

"I don't think a girl can escape puberty without meeting one or two or a dozen of those."

"I wish I could believe you were wrong about that."

She shrugged. "It's not all bad," she said, her gaze dropping to his shoulders—his chest—and lingering there. "Gives you the chance to discern between the good and the bad."

Which didn't mean a woman always was able to discern, he guessed, glancing again at that ring finger.

The guy, whoever he'd been, was a first-class fool. To lose a woman like this?

Chris drew himself up with a gulp of whiskey. Whoa. *It wasn't supposed to happen like this.* The words came again.

He was not one who entertained thoughts of having a relationship with a woman. His associations with women were just that—associations.

She reached for the top button on his shirt. "Do you mind if I undo this?" she asked, her other hand still holding the glass of wine he'd poured for her.

"No. Not at all." Chris's penis forced the words out of his mouth before his brain had a chance to react.

Her hand shook and her fingers caught and pulled a couple of strands of his chest hair as she struggled to open the button. The stiffness in his groin intensified. If she'd been experienced, assured, he might have had a hope.

He could have helped. Could have disrobed completely without a care. The sweet torment of Emma's soft skin scraping against his chest as she continued to try, one-handed, to get the button free from the hole had control of him.

Her attentions turned him on too much to deny himself. If the exquisite torture felt this good at the top buttons, he could hardly wait for her to tackle the buttons that were currently tucked into the fly of his dress slacks.

The wine sloshed a bit in the glass and she took a sip. The button was almost free and then she fumbled it and lost the ground she'd gained. She didn't giggle. Or sigh. Slowly, patiently, she tried again. Then finding success, she moved on to the next button.

He felt his underwear getting moist. He was going to have to stop her. Or help her. Or explode before he ever got a chance to show her any pleasure at all.

His shirt parted; she smiled a Mona Lisa smile, and Chris's body temperature grew.

He hadn't seen an inch of her flesh. Hadn't touched any private places. He hadn't even kissed her yet.

It wasn't supposed to happen this way.

HIS CHEST WAS glorious. She wanted to run her fingers through the abundance of dark crisp hair there—man hair.

Wow.

Chris groaned, and she glanced up. He was looking straight at her with a desperate plea in his gaze.

She jerked back. "What's wrong?" Had she hurt him? Had he changed his mind? Suddenly remembered a woman who was at home waiting for him? "You have a girl-friend, don't you?" She'd only asked if he was married. Rob wasn't married, either.

Dizzy with the effects of too much wine, she suddenly felt kind of sick.

"No, I don't."

His unequivocal answer sent a flash of re-lief through her entire body.

"And the only thing wrong is that I need to have you naked beneath me. I need to sink myself inside you and hear your cries of ec-stasy within the next few seconds or I'm going to be in paradise all by myself."

The wine dancing in her head again, she grinned. Hugely. "I have that effect on you?"

"Hell, yes."

Irrepressible delight coursed through her.

"I have no problem with your plan, then."

His eyebrows came together. "You're sure? I haven't prepared you."

She nodded and set her wine down on the table with a small splash, refusing to listen to a faint voice inside of her that wanted her to come to her senses. "I'm pretty sure you have," she said.

Chris's hand was at her crotch before Emma had any idea what he was going to do. He rubbed right where she was hottest. And then, without taking his eyes from her face, he had her slacks undone with one quick tug.

He kissed her, attacking her senses on multiple levels. His lips were firm, his tongue urgent as it entered her mouth. Emma grabbed for his neck, holding on tightly while he lifted her, undressed her some and lowered her back to the couch as he partially undressed himself.

"I have to get a condom." She barely understood the strained words. She saw him reaching back for his wallet and then she let go of him. But only long enough for him to slide the leather bifold from his back pocket, and find the foil packet tucked neatly in one corner.

With him suspended over her, she still had a chance to stop him. Her old self hovered above, watching what she was doing. Emma saw herself. But she didn't stop. Making love with Chris was the right thing to do. She was sure of it.

She felt no regret. None. At all.

She had to have him and that was all that mattered.

There was no hesitation in her body. No resistance. No discomfort at all. Emma's hips reached toward the force consuming her, welcoming him, urging him to fill her more deeply, with swifter thrusts. She had no idea who she was, or what she would be after this. She didn't care.

Driven by something inside of her, Emma gave herself over to the man on top of her. He was taking her away and she went willingly. Climbing higher and higher beneath him, with him. Becoming thinner and thinner until she burst into an explosion of sensation, saw stars and experienced wave after wave of the most incredible pleasure.

She'd had her first orgasm. And she wasn't the least bit sorry.

HIS BODY PULSED again and again, until he wasn't sure he could stand the glory of it. Chris cried out.

Oh, God. It wasn't supposed to happen like this. He was always in control.

And now he wasn't. He wanted more.

Gasping, sweating, he fell to Emma's side. He should be exhausted.

"Now, if you will allow me, I'll show you real pleasure," he drawled, hardly recognizing his voice. Without waiting for a response, he undid her blouse slowly, pausing after each button to run the backs of his fingers along the skin he was exposing.

She stared up at him, watching. "You want

me to stop?" he asked, remembering her earlier warning.

"No."

"You sure?"

"Absolutely." Her gaze didn't waver in spite of the tremble in her voice.

She moved her hips against him, sending another surge of blood along his muscle, pulling him in farther, and Chris had no choice but to take her at her word.

The woman wanted his loving and, God help him, he had to give it to her.

CHAPTER EIGHT

EMMA GAVE ROB a couple of extra hours to vacate her house on Saturday. She blamed her inability to get out of bed and leave the hotel room on her late night. It certainly wasn't a man keeping her there.

Her companion in crime was no more than a vivid memory. Sometime before dawn he'd kissed her one last time, told her to sleep, then, when she was more unconscious than not, he'd dressed and left. She hadn't even known his intent until she'd heard the latch on the door click behind him.

She'd risen then. In the restroom she'd found the note he'd left for her on the marble sink, telling her to stay as long as she liked. He'd arranged a late check-out. He told her to order breakfast on him.

"I hope that our night together is a memory that will last you a lifetime," he'd written. *"I know that I will never forget you. Chris."*

That was it. Just Chris. No last name. No

phone number. No way for her to contact him. No request for a way to contact her.

After reading the note half a dozen times Emma had told herself to dress, find her car and get the hell home.

And then she'd remembered Rob's deadline, which wasn't yet past, and had crawled back into bed. What the heck. Chris had presumably paid for the room. She might as well get some rest.

With the help of the wine she'd consumed the night before, she'd slept for several more hours—waking around noon to glasses half filled with stale wine and whiskey, the scent of lovemaking and her clothes in a neat pile on the table in front of the couch.

The note Chris had written was still there, too, crumpled on the bedside table. Right where she'd left it.

WITH HIS FADED orange coveralls stripped down to his waist, Chris dropped the wrench and swore. He was stranded on his boat about ten miles out. And saw a flash of long legs in his mind's eye.

At his father's insistence, he'd learned how to repair a boat engine before he'd pulled up his first trap. But there was only so much a guy could do to an engine with pistons that were done being overhauled. New rings weren't going to do it this time. He'd had no black smoke warning this time. Only a rough idle when he'd taken the boat out.

Maybe he'd have taken the engine coughs more seriously if he'd had any sleep. If he'd been able to wipe out the image of dark curls spread across his white pillowcase. He couldn't afford to miss another day's catch. And engine coughing could be healed after he'd brought in the haul. Usually.

At least he'd brought in a better than average catch. More than seven hundred pounds. At only three dollars a pound—less than half of what he used to sell for—he was going to gross twenty-one hundred. He could get the catch in to Manny. With the cost of running a lobstering operation coupled with his living expenses, he was going to be lucky to make this month's bills.

Which was another reason he didn't date. He couldn't afford to wine and dine a woman. He couldn't afford the time.

Forgoing the radio—and the coast guard— Chris pulled out his cell phone and dialed.

He couldn't afford a new engine, either. Or a day off work. He damn well couldn't afford to be distracted by thoughts of a woman—no matter how good the night before had been.

"Jim, it's Chris. I need a tow."

He gave his father's best friend his coordinates. Jim wasn't fishing anymore. He'd bought a new boat just before the economy failed and had lost it to bankruptcy a couple of years later. Now the sixty-seven-year-old fisherman drove a towboat for Manny.

If Chris couldn't find a way to fish and fix his boat at the same time, he could end up just like Jim.

"Be there in twenty," Jim told him, and hung up.

No questions asked.

EMMA PUSHED THE button on her car visor, activating the automatic garage-door opener at four o'clock Saturday afternoon and paused in the driveway. Rob's silver Ranger was still parked inside.

The tall, lanky, boyishly good-looking man came out of the kitchen and into the garage before the outer door was fully raised.

She had a choice. Back up and speed away. Or stay.

Emma pulled into her garage.

"You didn't change the locks." Rob was there, opening her door for her. "I spent the night praying that you'd give me another chance, Em. This was the first time since we got engaged," he said, his tone pleading. "I swear to you, it won't happen again. Ever."

She got out of the car, pulling her purse out with her.

"The look on your face, when you came in the bedroom yesterday…"

Emma made her way to the door and into the house.

"I will never forget that look, Em. Or forgive myself for putting it there."

He hadn't moved out. Everything was just as she'd left it the day before. Rob's shot glasses were on the second shelf of the window alcove over the sink. His espresso machine still sat on the counter. And his shoes were underneath the dining-room table—right where he always left them.

Most everything in the townhome—the furniture, the dishes, the mortgage—belonged to her. He'd sold his stuff when he'd moved in because they hadn't needed two of everything.

"You're in the same clothes you took with you yesterday."

She put her purse on the closet shelf. Not far from Rob's golf clubs. He was that sure of her.

She was that predictable.

"You have clothes at your mother's house."

She'd called her mother on her way home, letting Rose know that she'd stayed downtown and had a long rest. She'd assured Rose that she was fine and that she'd call her later. She'd opted out of joining her for dinner and a movie.

Now she wondered if maybe that hadn't been such a good idea. If she had someplace to be, something she had to do, she could leave without running away.

Chris had had all morning to contact her at his hotel room, but he hadn't. And he hadn't returned.

Unlike Rob, she knew when someone was giving her ample time to get out.

"You've been out all night."

Rob's tone turned accusing as he followed her into the living room, down the hallway and into their shared home office. She had no idea what she was going to do there, but it was a better choice than the bedroom, where she really wanted to be.

Or the shower, where she needed to be.

"Where were you?"

He was standing right behind her. Hounding her. Emma turned and stared him right in the eye. "That is none of your business."

"You've got a hickey on your neck."

Emma raised a hand to cover the mark.

She'd forgotten. Chris had been inside her—
for a second time—when she'd admitted that
she'd never had a hickey in her life. What
had been a hazy recollection crystallized
as though a high-powered beam had been
pointed at the memory.

"You were with another man!" The aston-
ishment in Rob's voice riled her. He didn't
have to sound so shocked. Like the idea of
another man wanting her was impossible to
imagine.

"You're no better than I am!"

He had that wrong. She'd waited until she
was free before she had sex with someone
else.

Rob reached out, taking hold of her shoulders, pulling her to him. "I'm sorry, Em. I
understand. And I forgive you. I'm actually
relieved." He looked down at her, a sympa-
thetic smile on his lips. "You don't know how
hard it's been living with someone as perfect
as you are. There's no way I could ever measure up. But now…"

"What do you mean, as perfect as I am?"

"You know!" He gave her shoulders a
squeeze. "You live completely on the white
side of black and white. You don't ever mess
up. Or do anything unless you know you
won't make a mistake. You have such high

standards you make it impossible for a guy
to live up to you."

Emma stepped back forcefully enough to
make him let go of her. She'd been crushed
that Rob had been unfaithful. He appeared
glad that she had been.

"Who was he, Em? Anyone I know?"

More nauseated than ever, Emma walked
out of the office. "Get out, Rob. Now. Take
your things and get out. The locksmith is on
his way."

"You don't mean that." He placed a hand
on her arm. Gently. "Please. Let's talk. We
can get through this. I know we can. I know
you, Em."

He did know her. Better than anyone ever
had. There was a lot of value in that. A lot
of worth.

Chris didn't know her at all. And didn't
want to.

If she let Rob leave, she'd be alone. Really
alone. Did she want that?

"Get out." The words came from deep
within. "The Lock Exchange guy is going
to be here soon. Whatever's still here by the
time the locks are changed, you lose."

"You don't know what you're doing."

"Yes, actually, I do." Emma shook inside,
scared to death but determined.

She'd done the unimaginable the night before. She'd left a bar with a man she didn't know. She'd shed her clothes for him, spread her legs for him. And then she'd been left to wake up alone.

Somehow she had to make something good come from that. She had to make the night count. She had to become a changed woman.

"I'm warning you, Em. If you do this, if you really force me out of here, I won't be back."

She stood still and tried not to cry.

"I mean it."

He took a step toward her.

"I know you mean it." Emma could hardly believe the firmness of her tone. "I am changing the locks and anything that's left behind, you lose. You've had twenty-four hours."

"Fine, then. But mark my words, you're going to regret this."

She faced him one last time, aware of how she must look in yesterday's clothes with last night's rumpled hair, smeared makeup and unbrushed teeth. "That's a chance I'm willing to take."

Emma didn't take chances.

But apparently the woman she'd unleashed the night before had caught a ride home with her.

CHAPTER NINE

CHRIS TOSSED BACK a few drinks with Jim at his house on Saturday night. The older man had taken a look at his boat and had verified what Chris already knew. He'd shot at least one piston. The *Son Catcher* wasn't going anywhere until Chris came up with a thousand bucks and the time to fix her.

And if he kept dipping into his savings, he wasn't going to have anything left for his retirement.

Not that he had any plans to quit working.

If he couldn't fish, there wouldn't be anything left to live for, anyway.

"You don't come around enough, Chris." Jim's wife, Marta, put a plate of fresh crab sandwiches on the table in the enclosed patio and pulled up a stool.

"I don't want to impose," Chris said.

"Your folks have been gone almost ten years, and you've been here, what, five times since then?"

It sounded so bad when she put it like that.

"I miss our Friday-night dinners."

Jim had been friends with Chris's father in high school. When they'd married, their wives had also become close friends. The two couples had shared dinner together every Friday night. And after Chris had been born, the only child among them, he'd become a part of the tradition. One that had continued until his parents' deaths.

After that, Chris found it easier to be alone.

EMMA SLEPT ON the couch Saturday night. With the television on.

She wasn't afraid of burglars. Or of the dark.

She was afraid of herself, that—alone in the queen-size bed, in the room that she'd shared for two years—she'd toss and turn and feel desperate.

She was afraid she'd do something crazy. Like call Rob. He'd be expecting a call. And, in spite of what he said, he'd come back.

She knew him well, too.

Another possibility, a worse one, was that she'd leave the house and go down to Citadel's. If Chris made his living there, he'd have to be there more than one night a week. Weekends were the biggest draw.

And if he was booked someplace else, Cody would probably know about that, too.

As badly as Emma wanted to see him again, she knew she shouldn't. So she didn't sleep much.

But she caught up on *I Love Lucy* reruns. And when dawn still took too long to arrive, she put in *Pillow Talk,* one of her favorite movies from her Doris Day collection. Emma owned every single movie Doris Day had ever made.

She loved them all.

Doris always got her guy. But she never lost sight of who she was in the process. Always remained true to herself.

She was an icon in her day, a woman before her time. The characters Doris depicted were strong women. Women who didn't need men to complete them, who were successful in their own right and found men to complement them.

Men who were so in love with her characters, that love changed them from playboys into faithful partners for life.

At seven in the morning, as the end credits of *Pillow Talk* played, Emma reached into the side-table drawer, pulled out a journal—an unused gift from one of her students—and opened it to the first page.

She wrote her name in large black print: *EMMA SANDERSON.*

And then she started a list.

1. I want to be loved by a man who loves me so much that that love changes him.

She waited for more to come to her, and when nothing presented itself, she closed the journal and put it back in the drawer. Then she went to take a shower and begin the rest of her life.

AT NINE O'CLOCK Sunday morning, Emma picked up the phone.

Ramsey Miller had given her Cal's number, after obtaining Cal's permission to do so. She'd programmed it into the contact list on her cell phone.

She'd let it sit there.

With the push of a button, she made another major life decision.

Her heart was pounding as she waited for Cal to pick up.

"Hello?"

His voice was deep. Distinguished.

"Hello?"

She almost hung up. She had no idea what she was getting into. What kind of Pandora's box she could be opening. What if the Whittiers tried to sue them?

"Hello?" Cal sounded more perplexed than irritated by the silence on the other end. The young boy she remembered had always been so patient with her and Claire. So willing to listen.

"Cal?"

"Yes?"

"It's Emma. Emma Sanderson. Detective Ramsey Miller told me that you said it was all right to call and…" *I'm a new woman now. Or at least I'm trying to be.*

"Emma. I wondered if that was you when I saw the area code and didn't recognize the number." There was hesitation in his voice. Not that she could blame him.

"I just… I called to apologize, Cal. I know that nothing I can say will ever make up for what happened to you—and to your father…."

When she'd been little she'd called Frank "Papa."

"You have nothing to apologize for, Emma. You were four."

"Over the years…I've thought of you. I could have called, but I didn't."

"You wouldn't have found a number."

"I might have. And if not, I should have

spoken up. Gone to the authorities. Told them that I didn't think your father did it. I should have been a friend to you, Cal. You were the best friend to me."

Her throat was dry. Each word was successively more difficult.

"No one was going to believe what you thought, Em. Not without some kind of proof to substantiate your belief. You were a kid. Frank was the only father you'd known. Of course you weren't going to believe the worst of him."

"I should have tried harder to convince Mom, instead of always supporting her."

"I can't speak to that," Cal said. "I've spent the past twenty-five years hating your mother."

"I don't blame you." What a bizarre conversation. There had been a time she'd never have believed she would ever talk to Cal again. And yet, sitting at the breakfast bar in her kitchen with tears in her eyes, she smiled. Feeling more at home than she'd felt in a very long time.

"I missed you so much. Not just at first, but over the years. I never stopped missing you."

"I missed you, too."

"You did?"

"Yeah, although it took me a while to admit it."

"What changed?"

"I've mellowed out a bit since I got engaged."

Emma's grin grew. "Who's the lucky woman?"

That started a conversation that lasted more than two hours. He told her about his fiancée, Morgan, and her ten-year-old son, Sammie. He also shared with her how much he enjoyed teaching American Literature and Creative Writing to college students. And then he brought the conversation back to Ramsey Miller. "He needs a DNA sample from Claire," Cal said. "That's why he originally went looking for the evidence box."

"I know." Emma hadn't told her mother about the DNA request, the reason for it. She hadn't told her about the missing evidence, either.

"Did Ramsey explain what was going on?" he asked quietly. "Do you know about Peter Walters?"

A feeling of dread settled in her stomach. "Yeah."

Detective Ramsey Miller had been on a case, tracking down a missing little girl. He'd followed a lead and found Peter Walters, the fifty-five-year-old kidnapper, and the toddler he'd abducted. Found them before Walters had been able to harm the girl. But, in Ramsey's words to Emma, she said, "It was clear that it hadn't been the bastard's first time at bat."

"Miller found things hidden beneath the floorboards in Walters's basement—items belonging to little girls. He's looking at all cold-case abductions on the East Coast and in the Midwest, testing DNA from the missing children, looking for a match. So far, he's positively identified four victims," Cal said softly.

"He told me that he found the stuff in the basement after a confession from Walters regarding what he'd done with one of the victims before and after he'd killed her."

A confession that, according to the detective, had made him puke.

"He thinks Claire might be the fifth." Emma's voice broke on the words. For so long now she'd prayed. On good days, she was able to picture Claire alive and well and happy—unaware that she'd been abducted.

"He's not sure, Em. From what I've gathered, Miller is trying to rule out victims as much as anything. When Claire was taken, DNA testing wasn't available. Now they can get samples of DNA from a twenty-five-year-old strand of hair. He just needs something of Claire's, something she touched or wore, to see if he can pull a sample. He wants to either rule Claire out as one of Walters's victims, or identify her and close her case."

That scared the hell out of Emma. What would she and Rose do if Claire's case was closed and their hope was unequivocally destroyed?

How did one go on without hope?

"He's not working alone on this," Cal continued. "There's a Detective Lucy Hayes, from Aurora, Indiana, who's helping him on the side, without pay. Miller gave me as many details as he could. According to him, he got in touch with Detective Hayes when he tried to check out a box of evidence pertaining to a cold-case abduction in Indiana and found it was already checked out. By her. He told me this only to reaffirm that he hadn't just been hounding my father. He wanted me to know that he's looking closely at every single case. It's like a quest for him. And apparently with this Hayes woman, too. They want to find Walters's victims, identify and track down Claire's abductor, to solve as many of these cases as they can."

She understood quests. It made her nervous as hell that someone else was exerting as much energy into her sister's case. Which made no sense. She needed to know what happened to Claire.

"There's something else, too," Cal continued softly, on the other end of the line. "Miller also wants to know why the evidence from Claire's case is missing. Walters couldn't have taken it. He's in prison. But did he have an accomplice? Or is there someone else out there involved in Claire's disappearance who wants to make certain there's never a chance of getting caught? When Miller called me, it was pretty clear he thought my father or I might have had something to do with the missing evidence."

The words dug at the hole in Emma's heart. "Oh, Cal, I'm so sorry. Even after all this time, to be hunted like a suspect…"

She and Rose had a lot to answer for. Too much to answer for.

"There's no way to make it better," she said aloud. "If I could change what we did—"

"I've made mistakes, too, Em. We all did. We did what we had to do to survive in the only ways we could see fit."

"You must hate us."

"I don't hate you."

But he'd said he hated her mother. And

while she loved Rose fiercely, would protect her fiercely, she couldn't blame Cal for hating her.

"I need to know who took that evidence, Em. Claire's DNA could lead us to answers separate and apart from the Walters case. Someone didn't want her evidence looked at for a reason."

"I know." She understood that he was asking her to give Miller what he wanted.

He was asking Emma to face the idea that her baby sister might have died at the hands of a fiend. That she might have suffered horrible atrocities.

"I've got the hair ribbons my mom used to put in our hair every day," Emma said. They were still in the wooden box they'd always been kept in. It was tucked away in the back of the closet in her office. "She never put ribbons in my hair again after that day."

Her mother had done everything she could to make certain that Emma was the plainest girl around. Not so unattractive to attract pity, just invisible, so that no one would notice her.

"If he can't lift any of Claire's DNA, he could get a sample of yours. It wouldn't be an exact match, but there'd be enough to identify one of the victims as a close relative of yours. Or not."

She didn't really have a choice to make. They all needed answers. Frank deserved answers. After being hounded for twenty-five years, just having his name cleared probably wasn't enough. The older man was probably not going to rest until he knew that the real culprit was caught and charged with the crime he himself didn't commit.

"I'll give the ribbons to Detective Miller. And a sample of my DNA if he needs it. I just need a little time. As badly as I need to know... I'm dreading... I mean, what if I find out my baby sister was—"

"Would you like me to go with you? I can fly up."

She wanted to accept Cal's offer.

"I'd like to, Emma. I know we won't get the results right away, but I don't want you doing that alone. Especially since I'm asking you to do it. It seems right that we go together."

She hadn't seen Cal in twenty-five years. Had never met him as a man. And yet, this was the big brother she'd lost at the same time her world had been blown apart. Right when she'd needed him most.

"I can't believe I'm saying this—I'm usually so capable—but would you?"

"Of course."

She wrapped her finger around a napkin. And watched it shake.

"Okay, good. When?"

In less than a minute, she had plans to see Cal in just over two weeks. He was in the middle of teaching an intercession class—a break in the college semester that allowed for special two-week classes—until then and wanted to be able to take a couple of days with her.

Just in case. He didn't say that. But she knew.

"You'll call me with your flight information?"

"I'll do better than that," he said. "Give me your email and I'll send you a copy of the itinerary."

She was committed. To finding out the truth.

And to seeing Cal again.

She was confronting the past that had taken away her present and future for long enough.

And she was still breathing.

"Weird how you still feel like family to me," she said, not quite ready to hang up.

"It's not so weird," Cal said. "We were an impressionable age when we were told we were going to be a family forever."

"You were the best big brother, Cal."

"You were easy to be nice to."

"Yeah, but I was a stupid girl...." She remembered one of Cal's playmates saying that about her once. She'd hated that boy after that. Hated Cal playing with him.

"Other than Dad, you and your mom and Claire were the only family I'd ever known."

His words hung in the air.

"Mom and I, it's always been just us." Whether the past was her fault or not, she felt responsible for at least part of his suffering. "Mom never, after your dad, after Claire... There's never been another relationship for her. She just works and goes home."

"That must be hard on you."

"Not as hard as it is on her." She wanted him to know that Rose's choices had not brought her happiness. That no one had won. Maybe, if he knew how much they'd suffered, he'd find a measure of justice in that, at least. "Remember that last day, how Claire sat on her knees on that chair at the table, with her bear in one hand, and shoved so many Cheerios into her mouth she choked?"

"Yeah. She said she was late and had to eat fast."

"She was always mimicking the rest of us," Emma said, brushing away a tear that dripped down her cheek.

"Like the time she answered the phone and told your mom's principal that she had to hang up because she had bills to pay?"

"I'd forgotten that!" Emma said with a grin, remembering. And wondering if Rose remembered. Then she said, "Mom still has that kitchen table. She'll never get rid of it."

"My father wants to talk to her." His tone dropped.

"You don't think that's a good idea?"

"He's lost a good portion of his life because of her. What do you think?"

"I think that our parents' lives are their own," Emma said slowly, saying words she'd never have said before. She couldn't protect Rose any more than Rose could protect her. "I think they need to do what they feel is right," she added.

"I'm not convinced."

"You might not have a choice."

"Meaning?"

"They're adults. And they were in love."

"She'd better not throw blame, or interrogate him, or—"

"Don't worry," Emma said, feeling a tremendous surge of love for the boy who'd grown into a man. "Mom feels even worse than I do about all of this, if that's possible."

"I just want you to understand that I won't tolerate any more blame cast on my father. Or any more slander. I'll take whatever means I need to."

"And I'll be right there fighting with you, Cal," Emma said. "Because right is right. And because, in spite of all the years and all the pain and sadness, the past couple of hours have reaffirmed that you're still my brother."

CHAPTER TEN

CHRIS WENT BACK to see Marta.

There was no reason for his visit. But Sunday, when he knew Jim would be at the bar with his cronies, Chris stopped by to see the woman who was his godmother, if one put any stock in that kind of thing. Chris never had.

She was sitting on the back patio with a cup of coffee when Chris pulled up.

"You came back," she said, opening the screen door to let him in.

He acknowledged the obvious with a nod.

"You still take your coffee black and as strong as God can make it?"

"Just like my dad." Chris had lost count of the number of times he'd heard how he drank his coffee just like Lyle Talbot had done. And, where coffee was concerned, he'd quit trying to be his own man.

While Marta went to the kitchen, Chris settled into the largest of the white wicker chairs facing the ocean in the distance.

He didn't need the view. He had a better one from home.

"I talked to Anne Havens at church this morning."

Anne and her husband, Trick, had been a couple of years ahead of Chris in school.

He didn't need to ask how they were doing. He'd just come from their house.

"She says Trick's having a rough go of it."

Trick had been the one to pull Wayne Ainge out of the water.

"He'll be fine."

"She was looking for someone to help out with Trick's boat until..." Marta looked him in the eye. She wouldn't tell him what to do—she wasn't as bold with him as his mother had been—but her expectations were clear.

"Already taken care of," he said, thinking about the conversation he'd just had with Anne.

Marta's approving smile went deeper than he'd have liked.

"You're a good boy, Chris."

He was no boy. And if he didn't quit thinking about long legs and dark brown curls, he wasn't going to be good for anything, either.

"I don't mean to be disrespectful, Aunt Marta—" Uncle Jim had become just plain

Jim around the first time Chris had worked a full day on his father's boat, but Aunt Marta was still his "aunt" "—but, the other night, about the fact that I don't come by as often as I should…"

"You took your folks' death hard, Chris. Everyone knew you would. It's understandable that you pulled away. I just hate that you still think you have to. You're not thirty anymore, son. If you don't start to open up, before long you'll be Jim's age and have no one but the guys at the bar to know if you're even alive or not."

"I'm not going to get married just so someone will know I'm not dead."

"I'm not talking about marriage. I'm talking about opening up to people. Letting them care about you."

She cared. And he'd hurt her. He read the pain in her eyes.

And he understood. Marta knew about the life of a fisherman. She'd accepted the dangers. The long hours. And she opened her heart to them, anyway. All she asked in return was that they love her back.

"I'm sorry."

"I know."

He should go.

"What's on your mind, Chris?"

What was niggling at him was nothing. He had more to do than there were hours in the day and night combined.

"The day my folks were killed," he said, and stopped when he saw the shadow cross Marta's face. "Do you know where they were headed?"

Or where they'd been?

"Yes."

"My mother told you?" He wasn't surprised. Marta and Josie Talbot had been best friends.

"Yes."

Marta would have sympathized. Women stuck together. She might even have encouraged Josie. At the very least she'd have understood.

Chris didn't.

Glancing at the older woman now, studying the lines on a face weathered from years of looking out to sea in hopes of seeing the right bow come up over the crest of the waves, Chris didn't blame her.

"I wasn't sure you knew," Marta said now.

Even though she was sitting at home alone this Sunday, there was no saying that as a younger, thinner, more attractive woman she'd been content to spend all those long hours alone.

"They'd just changed their wills. I was executor of both estates. And sole beneficiary, as well."

Graying eyebrows drawn together, Marta said, "I'd hoped they hadn't gotten that far. That at least their secret had gone to the grave with them."

Lyle and Josie had had a joint funeral—as husband and wife. They were buried side by side beneath the Talbot family marker in the seaman's graveyard in the middle of Comfort Cove.

The plot of land that divided the real town from the more upscale tourist district.

The plot that divided Chris's life. In so many ways.

"You've known all these years, and yet you never said anything."

The only response he had to give was a shrug.

"You blame her."

His mother had been named as the plaintiff.

"I know that my father would never, ever have left her." Or turned his back on her, no matter what she'd done. Lyle had loved Josie more than he'd loved any other human being on earth.

"She spent the majority of her life alone, Chris."

He knew that. Women who married full-time fishermen often did.

"When you were little, it wasn't so bad, but once you got older, and joined your father on the boat…"

So this was his fault?

"Some people like time to themselves. Josie never did. Her head played tricks with her. She'd start to imagine problems at sea, imagine the phone call telling her that she'd lost both your father and you."

Out of respect for Marta, Chris forced himself to stay seated, but he didn't need to hear any more.

"You were about three months old when she had her first panic attack. She called me, unable to breathe, certain that she was having a heart attack."

Fingers clenched around the arms of his chair, the wicker punching a pattern in his skin, Chris stared out at the ocean—the only mate he was ever going to have.

"I called 9-1-1…."

His gaze swung to Marta. "I never heard about a 9-1-1 call." He'd never heard about the panic attacks, either, but then he'd only really ever had one interest—the sea. Which was why he was still single at forty.

"She didn't want me to say anything to Jim or your father."

"And you did as she asked?" If his mother had a problem, Lyle had had a right to know.

"I rode with her in the ambulance and was there with her when she saw the doctor. He said she was just suffering from panic and that she had to get a hold of herself. Back then panic attacks weren't seen as legitimate physical ailments. They were considered the result of mental weakness. There were drugs that tranquilized but no medications prescribed to help control the chemicals in the brain that trigger them."

"And that's why she didn't want Dad to know. Because she didn't want him to think she was…mentally lacking."

"Right."

He could understand that. Sort of. Surely, if his mother and father had shared any kind of real closeness, as a husband and wife should, then she should have been able to trust Lyle with the information.

To know that he loved her enough to stand by her, to help her if she needed it.

"I'd hoped that hearing from the doctor that she had the ability to control her emotions, to control how she reacted to things, would help her get better, but it didn't. That day just escalated her panic. What if she'd really been having a heart attack? There'd have been no way to reach your father—and you were so little and helpless. She'd have died alone and left you alone, too."

So his mother had chosen to insure that she wasn't alone? Was he expected to believe that she'd just been staving off panic all those years she'd cheated on his dad?

Chris didn't know. He wasn't sure he wanted to know. He'd wasted enough time. Women were women. He was a lobsterman. And he had work to do.

Standing, he took one sip from the cup of coffee Marta had made for him, and bent to kiss her on the cheek.

"Thank you."

"I'm always here, Chris. Anytime you want to talk."

"Yeah." He turned toward the door. "I'll be better about stopping by."

"Jim and I love you like you were our own son, you know that."

He couldn't just walk out on her. Swinging around, he met her gaze. "I know," he said. "I love you, too, Aunt Marta."

The words didn't stick as badly as he might have expected.

Probably because he spoke the truth.

EMMA WENT TO work. She visited her mother—telling Rose that she'd spoken with Cal Whittier, but mentioning nothing about Cal's imminent trip or Ramsey Miller's investigation—and during all of the empty hours she had she rearranged her house.

Rob's desk went to charity right along with the clothes and shot glasses he'd left behind. If he thought that she was going to come to her senses, that he would be back, he was wrong. Her sewing machine got a new table and was set up opposite her desk, and a Peg-Board went up above the machine to hold an array of colorful threads. What used to be merely an office was now a sewing room, too.

By Wednesday, she still wasn't sleeping well. She'd moved from the couch to the bed that was now on the opposite wall. She put in old movies to lull her to sleep. At three in the morning, she redid lesson plans and graded papers.

She tried not to think about Chris. She tried not to let her body remember the sensations he'd evoked. When she started to respond physically to things she wasn't thinking about, she decided to use her quilting skills to make a wall hanging and spent time on the internet familiarizing herself with all sorts of quilting patterns.

On Thursday night, finding herself on the couch, irritated with television commercials and no longer distracted by movies, she pulled out the journal again. Just to see what she'd written.

1. I want to be loved by a man who loves me so much that that love changes him.

She stared at the words. She'd written them down because, in that moment, she'd felt them so strongly. Now, days later, she felt the same way.

She grabbed her pen.

2. I want to be brave enough to live my life to the fullest.

She read what she'd written again. And reread it several times. If there was going to be any value in this exercise, she had to be completely honest.

And she realized that, like it or not, her resolutions were about Chris.

Holding the page between her thumb and forefinger, she started to tug gently, planning to tear out the page so that its removal wouldn't show. She could make the journal appear brand-new. Just as it had been before.

The first thread gave way and she stopped. Closed the book. Put it carefully back in the drawer, in the space allotted to it. Returned the pen to its rightful spot. And went to bed.

EMMA MEANT TO make plans for Friday night. But she'd had a dance-club meeting to officiate after school and hadn't known what time she'd be through. She hadn't known how hungry she'd be, or whether or not her mother would want to spend the evening with her.

Other than her daily phone calls to see how Emma was doing, Rose was giving Emma space. It was a first, and she appreciated it. But eventually her mother was going to want to see her.

Eventually she'd have to tell Rose about Detective Miller's investigation. The detective had agreed to contact her first, before contacting Rose, but she didn't want to have to tell Rose at the last minute. Still, she felt she needed more time to herself before she got around to that.

It had been exactly one week since Emma

had decided to change her life, and here she was, in her car, driving away from school toward a long weekend filled with fabric squares.

She would not panic.

And she most definitely would not drink. The new Emma was not to be trusted. She had some maturing to do before she got the reins again.

Her cell phone barely got half a ring in before Emma pushed the green button to answer the call.

"Hello?" Pulling into a lot not far from the high school, Emma put her car in park.

"Em? I've missed you, sweetie. How are you?"

Damn. That's what she got for not checking caller ID.

"I'm fine, Rob." *Hang up. Hang up. Hang up.* "How are you?"

"Not fine at all. I can't get a handle on a life that doesn't include you, Em. Nothing tastes right. Nothing feels right."

Don't care. Don't care. Don't care. "Did you find a place to stay?"

"No. I've got my things in storage and I'm at that little motel around the block from the office." He spoke to her as though they were still together. With the warmth that spoke of lifelong partnership. "I've looked at some houses, but I don't know. I just keep thinking that those cupboards won't work because your Pfaltzgraff, stoneware and Corelle won't fit. Or the space for the refrigerator isn't big enough for our side-by-side."

My side-by-side. I bought it.

"Or the kitchen will be perfect but the master closet won't have room for all of your jackets. And then I wasn't sure you'd like the neighborhoods. One was too new. One was older, like you like, but I thought you'd think the houses more run-down than finely aged."

Her townhome was finely aged. Sixty years old, with updated wiring and plumbing, but original hardwood floors—even on the stairs—and white, solid-wood slated cabinets.

Breath caught in her throat. She was all alone. And she didn't need to be.

The world was filled with male sharks. Rose had driven that fact home to Emma from the time she was seven and had a crush on a boy in her class.

Rob was not a shark.

An occasional philanderer, yes. But he knew Emma. Really knew her. He paid attention to her likes and dislikes. More than she'd ever realized and…

"What do you want, Rob?"

"To see you, of course. To make our life right again. I want to come home, Em."

Her beautiful old home awaited her. Rearranged to her taste. And devoid of him.

"We've already been—"

"Let's just meet for drinks," he said. "Let's see each other. Talk. Then if you still feel like you don't want me back, I'll move on."

She'd already given away his desk. His shot glasses. She'd thrown out the extra razor blades he'd left in the linen closet. Cleared him out of her house.

Had she made a mistake? Been too hasty?

She'd slept with another man.

And he'd left her alone in a hotel room with no way to contact him.

Looking down at her tan slacks and low-heeled pumps, the turquoise silk blouse she'd worn to work that day—an outfit Rob had picked out for her—Emma wondered if she should just quit fighting and accept herself as she was. Rob apparently did.

She stared out at the parking lot and gave in to the inevitable. "Can you be at the Dragon in ten minutes?" The lounge wasn't far from her house. They'd met there for dinner many times after work before going home together.

"Give me fifteen and you're on."

CHAPTER ELEVEN

EMMA DROVE AROUND the block several times. She was not going into another lounge to sit alone. Not even for five minutes. As soon as she saw Rob's silver Ranger pull into the lot, she circled one more time and parked.

He was waiting at a table for two in the shadowed back half of the room where they'd be least interrupted, overheard or even noticed.

The type of table Emma always chose.

A glass of white zinfandel sat in front of the empty seat. Rob had a vodka and orange juice in his right hand as she walked up.

He stood. Pulled out her chair. Leaned in for a kiss and, when she turned her head, kissed her on the cheek. He held her hand as she sat down. And brought it with him to the top of the table.

"It's good to see you, babe. I've missed you."

She'd missed him, too. But was it because he was Rob? Or because sitting at a quiet, obscure table and having your favorite wine waiting for you felt normal, and normal felt safe? Still she said, "It's good to see you, too."

He'd been a part of her life for a long time. A partner to her in many ways.

"I called Cal Whittier," she told him almost as soon as she sat down. She'd been bursting with the news and had no one to confide in.

"Oh, Em! How'd it go? Was he civil to you, I hope?"

"Better than that," she said, smiling at him—a real smile that she felt all the way to her frozen core. "Crazy as it sounds, it was as if we were kids again. I felt...close to him. Like I did then. Like he really was my brother just as we believed back when we were young."

"What about him?" Rob's gaze was piercing, protective. "Do you think he felt the same?"

"I know he did. Rob, he's coming to Comfort Cove. He's going to come with me to the police station to drop off the box of hair ribbons."

"So you decided to give Ramsey the DNA?"

Rob had been insistent that it was the right choice. Emma had been the one wavering.

"Yes. If he can't get Claire's, I'll give him

mine. It won't be an exact match, but it could be close enough."

He smiled. "Good for you, Em. I'm proud of you."

Tilting her head, she asked, "Why?"

"Because it's a big step for you. A potentially painful move."

She recognized the woman he was describing. Saw her clearly. And didn't like the image.

He took her other hand, holding both of them between his. "This is what I've always wanted for you, Em. To be able to do what you know is right without fearing the consequences."

"Fear serves a purpose," she said. "It protects you from danger."

"Yes, in the case of jumping out of an airplane without a parachute, or walking into a dark alley alone. But it also prevents you from experiencing so much of life."

Like spending the most sensual, unforgettable night in the arms of a man she didn't know?

Or waking up alone the morning after?

"Where'd you go just now?" Rob was frowning.

Shaking her head, Emma pulled one hand free, and took a sip of her wine. After a week

of abstinence to recover from her overindulgence, the sweet liquid tasted good. Felt nice
and warm going down.

"So will I get to meet Cal when he's in
town?" Rob asked. "I'd really like to."

Part of her wanted him to.

"I…"

Rob's phone rang. Still holding her hand,
he pulled the cell phone out of his case,
looked at the blinking screen and said,
"Sorry, hon, I have to take this.

"Look, Tiffany, I told you, don't keep calling me," he said into the phone.

Tiffany. Emma felt completely blank. On
the inside and out.

"What happened last week was a mistake.
A huge mistake. The biggest of my life. I love
Emma. I'm sorry."

Last week. Tiffany was the woman in her
bed? And he'd taken her call? Now?

As the woman on the other end of the line
said something, Emma pulled her remaining
hand away from Rob's.

The alarm in his eyes as he stared at her,
pleaded with her, was too reminiscent of
other times he'd had to face up to his indis-
cretions.

"If you call me again, I'm going to block
your number," Rob said next.

Emma wondered why he hadn't already done it.

Had he been keeping that window open in case her door remained firmly shut?

"Thanks for the wine. I have to go." Gathering her purse, Emma stood, leaving Rob to work things out with Tiffany, and walked out of the restaurant.

CHRIS WORKED UNTIL his shoulders ached and his knuckles were scraped and bleeding.

And then he did something he rarely did.

He bought a bottle, took it down to the *Son Catcher* with him, anchored down in a cove just below his house and drank just enough to put him to sleep.

RAGING AT HERSELF this time, more than at the man who couldn't be faithful if his life depended on it, Emma found the courage to be brave.

Her desire to break the chains that had bound her to Rob took her out of that restaurant and back to her car.

If she wasn't happy, she had only herself to blame. She got what she'd asked for. Because she didn't ask for enough for herself.

She was the one letting herself down.

Spurred by Rob's phone call, by the fact

that he'd recognized the number and taken the call because he somehow thought Emma would understand, Emma drove to the tourist district.

What if Chris had been thinking about her this week? What if their night together had lingered in his mind as it had in hers?

He had no way of finding her. No way of tracking her down. She'd paid cash for her wine last Friday night. She'd told Chris her first name, and nothing else about herself.

She'd been a woman with no previous identity. No past.

Emma parked the car in the lot across from Citadel's and marched across the street.

She paused on the sidewalk, trying to see in, to see the bar and the piano dais—or more accurately, to see who was sitting there.

She could make out a few shadows at the bar and nothing else. The streetlights were too bright, and the interior of Citadel's too dim, for her to see who sat at the piano. With a pounding heart, Emma pulled open the door.

Citadel's was crowded. Piano music filled the room. From what Emma could see, all of the dining tables were occupied so she didn't approach the host to be seated.

Still, she couldn't just stand there.

And there was an empty stool at the bar. Less than a minute after she sat down, Cody was standing in front of her with a bottle of wine in hand and his eyebrows raised in question.

She nodded. What the hell.

She'd always liked wine. And she'd read an article this week—while she was checking on the effects of overindulgence after her night of craziness—about how a glass of red wine a night was actually healthy for women. The grape seed extract in red wine was reportedly a powerful antioxidant that was good for the heart among other things.

When Cody placed the glass in front of her, she picked it up and sipped.

Her movements were calculated. She had it all planned out.

After her third sip, she glanced over at the piano. But she already knew Chris wasn't there.

The music was good. Really good. But it wasn't art.

So she waited.

She was going to stay uptown again tonight. But she was going to get her own room. And stay sober. No more foolishness. She was going to take a long hot soak in a tub. And make certain she wasn't home if Rob tried to contact her again.

She knew he would, and she didn't want to deal with him tonight.

Tonight was for her.

"He's not coming tonight."

Jumping in her seat, almost tipping over her wineglass, Emma looked at Cody. The bartender had appeared in front of her again without her being aware of him. He stood, shining a glass with a white towel, and she was pretty certain he was pitying her.

"Who?"

"Chris."

She considered pretending that she didn't know what Cody was talking about and concocting some story about how she was waiting for someone to join her. Or about coming back for the music.

The actions of a coward.

"He told you that?"

"He called."

"I hope everything is okay."

"Yeah, it's not very often that he misses a Friday."

"And he didn't say why he was missing tonight?"

"No, but then he doesn't generally let us

know if he isn't going to be here to play. All the pianists are here on a voluntary basis."

"Then why did he call?" *Because of her?*

"Because he's bringing an extra catch in the morning for a private party the owner's hosting tomorrow night." Cody didn't point out that it was none of her business.

"An extra catch?" she asked.

"Of lobster."

She'd only had three sips of wine on top of the half glass she'd consumed at the Dragon, and yet she felt as if she'd stepped into a slow-motion film. "I don't understand."

"Chris is a lobsterman. Didn't he tell you?"

"A lobsterman?"

"Yeah. I thought he'd have told you or I wouldn't have said anything. You know, last week... I thought the two of you were hooking up."

Grabbing the bottle of wine, he tilted it over her nearly full glass, topping it off. "I'm really sorry, ma'am," Cody said. "I assumed you were here to see Chris again and..."

Emma smiled. "No problem," she said. "I'm just here for the music."

Chris was a fisherman. From the local docks. Her mother had forbidden her to frequent them. For very good reasons.

Far more than being a danger to her libido,

Chris was a dangerous man. In a dangerous profession.

Cody had just saved her from herself.

With that thought, Emma ordered a soda and, an hour later, ordered a third. But not until after she'd left the bar long enough to secure a room for herself at the inn next door—a less-expensive family establishment, *not* the glitzy place Chris had taken her to.

She'd nurse her pop. She'd hang out at Citadel's until bedtime. She'd show them all that she really was just there for the music.

And then she'd go sleep off another Friday night in the tourist district.

"Hey, Beautiful, how's life?"

"Life's just peachy, Chris. How's my favorite guy doing?"

"Great. Things are great." He was leaning against the bow of the *Son Catcher,* the fourth Saturday in September—two weeks after he'd left a beautiful dark-haired woman in a hotel room. Holding a half-empty bottle of orange soda, Chris peered past the dock to the ocean that had come between him and Sara. "Got the engine overhauled. Replaced the pistons to the tune of a thousand bucks."

"Thank God. I was getting kind of tired of

hearing you whine about the damned thing.
How long did it take?"

"Couple of weeks."

"Whoa!"

He held the phone away from his ear as
Sara Bailey yelped. "You went a couple of
weeks without fishing?" Incredulity turned
to sobriety as she asked, "What's the matter
with you?"

"Nothing's wrong with me. I'm fit as a
fiddle and as ornery as ever."

"You don't have an ornery bone in your
body, Christopher Michael Talbot. Now tell
me what's wrong. And don't give me any
bullshit. I know you, remember? I'm the
woman you were going to promise to love
and cherish until death did us part. The one
who lost out to those damned lobsters of
yours. There is no way in hell you'd miss
two weeks of fishing before the snow hits."

"I didn't miss fishing, smarty-pants," he
said with a swig of soda and a grin, and then
he sobered, too. "We lost a man a few weeks
back, a young kid from Alaska who'd signed
on with Trick Havens. Havens was there,
tried to save the kid, but couldn't get to him
in time. He's pretty shook up. Anne called
and asked if I could help fill his orders for a

bit so I made a deal with her. I'd fish for both of us if I could use his boat."

"You've been bringing in two hauls?"

"I've had some help." Havens had the money to hire hands, even with the low prices Manny was paying. Trick's father-in-law dabbled in things Chris didn't want to know about.

"And you've been working on the *Son Catcher* every day after hauling in two loads?"

"Utility lights work wonders."

"You been sleeping at all, Chris?"

"Enough." Hard work had always cured whatever ailed him. Far more than lying sleepless on a mattress staring at the ceiling had ever done.

"I worry about you."

"Don't."

"Too late." She sighed and, picturing the way she curled those full lips up to her pert little nose any time she was exasperated, he grinned again. "I assume you're calling to tell me that you won't be coming for Thanksgiving or Christmas again this year," she said next. She'd texted him the week before about the holidays.

"Wrong." He might need to take her up on the invitation. Though why he would after years of saying no, he couldn't fathom. "I'm calling to find out if that man of yours has an extra connector rod around his shop." He named the specifics for his thirty-year-old engine.

Sara's husband—a colonel in the air force who, as a hobby, rebuilt and refurbished old engines—was known to enthusiasts all over the country and made a mint dealing parts.

"A little too much torque in your wrench, sailor?"

"Put Jeff on, would you?"

"He's out with Lily, teaching her to fly his new helicopter."

Chris's foot dropped from the rail to the deck of the boat. "She's only four," he said. "You really think that's a good idea?"

"It's a remote-control toy I bought him for his birthday." Sara chuckled. "Listen to you, Chris, sounding all protective and unclelike."

"She's the only kid left in my family," he said. And not technically even that. He wasn't Lily's uncle by blood or marriage. Just by insistence from her parents, who considered themselves his family.

"Have Jeff call when he gets in, will you?" he said, frowning at the lights of a couple of boats bobbing out on the dusky horizon. He resented them. Because he wasn't out there with them.

"Of course. And don't worry, Chris, if he doesn't have the part, he'll find it and over-night it to you."

He was counting on it. He got ready to hang up. And then, watching those boats, he blurted, "I'm thinking of selling the house."

"What?" Another squeal he didn't need. "You were born in that house," she said. "Your father was born in that house. It's the most prime real estate in Comfort Cove."

His house was prime real estate by de-fault, not by money. The place was one of the original buildings in the area, built be-fore Comfort Cove was even a village. And when ordinances had been passed to prevent erosion of the coast, forbidding the construc-tion of any buildings within two acres of the ocean, his family home had been grandfa-thered in. It sat alone, at the top of the cliff that signified to boaters that they were reach-ing Comfort Cove.

"What do I need a three-bedroom house for? I'm hardly there."

"It's your home, Chris. You are absolutely not going to sell it."

He watched the lights on the ocean.

"I could use the money to buy a new engine for the *Son Catcher,* a cabin cruiser to live on, pay off my truck and have enough left over for a comfortable savings account."

"Live full-time on the ocean? Over my dead body, Christopher Talbot. You already give enough of yourself to the bitch that stole you from me. You will not sell that glorious house and let her take the rest of you."

He considered what she said.

The house might be too much for him, yet those walls, the memories and voices they held, were all the family he had left.

Or would ever have.

But thinking about getting out sure beat sitting in the dark listening to the silence his folks had left behind.

CHAPTER TWELVE

EMMA HAD DINNER with her mother three times the week following her return visit to Citadel's, and while they talked openly about Rob's exodus from her life, Emma didn't mention Cal's impending visit.

Emma mentioned Chris, the fisherman, to no one.

She bought fabric for a floral quilt in bright colors for her bed and, as an afterthought, added fabric for matching pillow shams. She'd never made them before, but she'd started a wall hanging that was shaping up nicely. She was brightening her home, if not her life.

Rob called daily until she was tempted to block his number, but didn't, as she didn't want to suffer the backlash. And when his emails started showing up in her in-box, she read the first one to make sure he didn't have a legitimate reason for contacting her, and then deleted the rest without reading them.

On Saturday night, Cal sent her his flight

itinerary. He'd be arriving Monday just after four. She was picking him up straight from school. They were going to have dinner with Detective Miller and then he'd catch the red-eye back. He'd booked a changeable flight and could afford to stay longer if Emma needed him. Emma couldn't sit still, thinking about seeing him again after so many years. For so long she'd clung to the memory of him, of her big brother, drawing strength from the past. Would having him in her life in the flesh be as good as the memory? Or would she find that she'd clung to something that wasn't really there?

Would he be disappointed in her? A woman who'd spent her entire life playing it safe, because of the danger inherent in taking risks?

On Sunday, she paid her bills. Made out her grocery list, shopped and put away the week's supplies. She ate a healthy lunch. Walked on the treadmill in her spare bedroom—purchased because it wasn't safe for a woman to walk in the park alone—and then, after sewing for a bit, tried to read.

Camilla pulled the knife from her sock.

Words bounced on the page, morphing into an image of Chris's face. Of Cal as a boy. Of Claire. Chris's face. Cal. Claire.

Cal and Claire she could understand. They mattered.

But why couldn't she let go of Chris?

It was his eyes. When he looked at her it was as if he saw things inside her that no one else ever saw. She hadn't shown them to him. He'd just seemed to know.

He was a man from the docks. She was imagining things.

Camilla pulled the knife from her sock.

Rose had warned her about fishermen. Rose had fallen for one once. Which was why Emma and Claire hadn't had a father until Frank Whittier had come into their lives.

Their biological father had married Rose, but he'd cared more about the sea than he had about his family. And when he'd had a chance to apprentice in Alaska with the promise of owning his own boat, he'd left them.

Unfortunately for him, he'd taken up with another man's woman shortly after arriving in Alaska. A man who hadn't been so ready to give up his wife.

Camilla pulled the knife from her sock.

Everyone knew that fishermen were all alike. Rugged and coarse. They were drinking men who spent their days fighting waves that could kill them in an instant. Men who weren't available when you needed them.

Stop it already.

Emma stared at the book she held—a light-hearted adventure novel she'd been looking forward to for months.

Camilla pulled the knife from her sock.

Who was Camilla?

She stared. White and black piano keys appeared in her mind's eye. Strong fingers coaxed beautiful music from them. Just as they'd later played all over her body...

Chris's fingers had been clean, manicured. Nothing like the dirty fisherman's hands Rose had warned her about.

She'd had sex before. Why in the heck couldn't she put that one night behind her? Why did every taste and smell from that night linger in the deepest recesses of her being?

Camilla pulled the knife from her sock.

Emma had no idea who Camilla was, why she had a knife in her sock or even why she was wearing socks.

"I'm sorry," she said aloud, offering her regrets to her favorite author as she put the book down on the table beside her.

The table with the drawer that held her journal.

Pulling the drawer open, she removed the leather-bound book and read the two lines she'd written.

1. I want to be loved by a man who loves me so much that that love changes him.
2. I want to be brave enough to live life to the fullest.

Emma put the journal away and stood up from the couch.

Clearly she'd made a huge mistake in going to Citadel's the night she'd caught Rob with Tiffany. She'd entered a dangerous world and it was time to get herself out of it—for once and for all.

Grabbing her purse, she didn't even look at herself in the mirror, let alone stop to put on makeup or fix her hair. In her blue cotton slacks, loose-fitting sleeveless blouse and expensive flip-flops, she was not dressed for the seamier side of town. But she was going there, anyway.

She was going to find Chris and quit romanticizing or fantasizing, or whatever the heck she was doing.

She'd made a mistake; she would learn from it. She was not going to let it trap her at home.

Someplace out there was a life with her name on it. Waiting for her.

She just had to be brave.

CHRIS WENT FISHING on Sunday, making it his fourteenth day in a row on the water pulling up double traps. Because it was Sunday, he was on Trick's boat alone. Hired hands could afford to take an occasional day off.

And because his conversation with Sara the day before had coughed up more issues than he wanted to give time to, he was tired, too. But he brought in a better than average catch, sold the entire take to Manny, bedded Trick's boat down for the night and still had several hours of daylight to give to the little engine that could.

Jeff was sending him the part he needed—it was due to arrive by special courier later that day. He was going to be ready to drop it into place the second it arrived. And if all went well, he'd be back on the *Son Catcher* later that week. He hoped to God that Trick was ready to get back to work, as well.

Not that he minded the extra work—or extra money—Trick's absence brought him. What he minded was that one of the brotherhood was at odds with the ocean.

In the denim shorts and stained gray T-shirt he'd worn under his coveralls, he was up to his elbows in grease and stepping out of the galley when he saw her. He stepped back quickly—his ages-old deck shoes saving him from falling on his ass as he nearly missed the stair.

The string of curse words he softly emitted didn't take the sting off the anxiety he felt.

At Citadel's the night before, after he'd unloaded the owner's order, he'd shared a beer with Cody. The bartender had been on break and asked to have a word with him.

The woman, Emma, had been in there looking for him the week before. Cody had said more than he would have except that he'd assumed she already knew what Chris did for a living, and he'd been meaning to apologize for the indiscretion. Bottom line was, she knew where to find him.

Cody had said something else, too. Emma had seemed uneasy. She'd ordered wine but hadn't taken more than a few sips, at which time she'd switched to soda.

What woman spent hours at a bar on a Friday night drinking soda?

She hadn't asked the right questions for a woman trying to check up on a guy she might want to make it with. Like did he meet women there often. Or did he have a special woman. No, she'd said she was there for the music.

Cody thought she'd been looking for Chris.

In his experience, a woman did that only if she wanted something from him.

But what could she possibly want from him? He hadn't left anything behind in the hotel room, had he?

Maybe she was coming back for more. There was always that chance—which was a good reason for Chris to avoid her.

Standing below, sweating, listening for her approach, Chris swore again.

Three sips of wine, Cody had said. From a woman he'd known to consume many, many glasses.

And now she was here. At the docks. Looking for him.

As far as he knew, there was only one reason a woman quit drinking. And looked up a man with whom she'd recently had sex.

A long time ago, Sara had refused a glass of wine he'd poured her, the time she'd been afraid they'd made a baby. She'd also broken their engagement shortly after his horrified reaction to her news.

Just as soon as she'd started her period.

She hadn't wanted to be married to a man who would willingly take on the dangers of the ocean even when he might leave behind a fatherless child. She hadn't wanted to marry a man who found the thought of being the father of her child so distressing.

It had been the beginning of an end, and that refused glass of wine had started it all.

Could Emma be pregnant? His absolute worst nightmare. Something that scared him more than death.

Flashbacks from their night together haunted him. The long-legged part. The moments when he'd felt like he could fly without a plane—and the part where he'd used the same condom twice because he hadn't taken it off before they started in again and he hadn't had a second one to use.

He could not be a partner. He could not be a husband. And he most definitely could not be a father.

"CAN I HELP you?"

The man had a definite paunch, but otherwise looked exactly like the stereotypical fisherman her mother had described. *Manny,* his tag read. He looked old enough to have been around the summer Rose had hung out at the docks.

Whether Manny had known the boat hand who'd hired on with a local fisherman more than twenty-nine years ago, Emma didn't know. And she didn't care. She had no intention of speaking to the man about her father.

"I'm looking for Chris. Do you know which boat is his?"

"If you mean Chris Talbot, yeah, I know. What do you want with him?"

Talbot. Piano man had a last name.

Turning away from Manny, she caught a glimpse of movement down at the dock. On a boat. A figure appeared briefly. So briefly she almost missed it.

But she hadn't missed the ragged, dirty clothes. The machine parts strewn around the boat.

And she hadn't missed the face.

"Uh, nothing," she said. "Sorry to bother you." She backed down the sidewalk, away from the marina store, leaving Manny standing outside on the stoop, and headed to her car as rapidly as she could without breaking into a run.

Heart pounding, feeling sick to her stomach, she started the car and sped away.

The one time she tread dangerously, the *one* time, and she had to have sex with a *fisherman?*

Her mother would have a stroke if she knew.

CHAPTER THIRTEEN

CHRIS WAS A MAN of honor. When a man's life depended on an entity like the ocean, duplicity didn't much pay. And when his sole companion was his conscience, the only way to keep the relationship stable was to get along with it.

Which was why he called in another favor. He had a couple of police-officer acquaintances who were lobster lovers. They'd been purchasing fresh catch directly from Chris for years. In exchange, they drove by to check on his house occasionally while he was out on the water.

On Monday, they did a little detective work for him. Manny's surveillance camera had recorded an image of Emma's car in the lot. The license plate was clearly visible. By the time Chris finished work for the day, the woman who wouldn't get out of his mind had a last name. Sanderson. And an address, too. She didn't have a landline, only a cell phone, and it was unlisted. His law-enforcement friends drew the line at passing along what was, technically, privileged information.

Any private eye could have ferreted out the information they did turn over. Just not as quickly.

At that moment, Chris was all about getting it done. If he had a potentially life-altering problem, he needed to tend to it immediately.

CAL'S FLIGHT WAS late. Waiting inside the terminal, just beyond the secured arrival gate, Emma realized what it meant to shake in her shoes. She was a nervous wreck. How was she going to recognize him? She should have brought a sign, told him what color she'd be wearing. Something. She hadn't thought of it. This was Cal. She'd once lived with him.

He wouldn't know her, either.

And what if Detective Miller's suspect was Claire's abductor? What if this day became one of those days that forever altered her life?

She needed to know what had happened to her baby sister. Finding Claire had been her life's purpose since the day she had gone missing. Emma needed closure. But to go to bed at night without hope of ever seeing Claire again? For so long that hope had been the source of her strength. She was Claire's big sister. She had to hold on.

She had to believe.

And what about Rose? Could her mother survive without hope? Without purpose?

With a twinge of guilt, thinking of her mother's reaction were she to know what Emma was doing right then, Emma peered through another throng of travelers exiting the gate.

She just had to spot a man standing around with no one to meet him.

She had to quit thinking about the old wooden box of ribbons in her bag. She was doing the right thing.

She was not making another big mistake.

Cal was a brother to her. She hadn't asked to have him move in with them all those years ago. She hadn't asked to love him.

Cal had done no wrong to her or her mother. Neither had Frank, for that matter. Just the opposite.

The passageway cleared. Emma paced, all but oblivious to the others waiting to collect loved ones. There was a young man with flowers, watching the hall down from the gates.

More people flooded the passage, held up

by an older, heavyset woman who probably should have asked for a wheelchair.

And then she saw him. In the middle of a mass of people pulling carry-on bags, wearing backpacks and talking into their cell phones, was Cal. He was taller than she'd expected. His hair was darker and his face shadowed with whiskers, but his eyes were all Cal. And they were trained on her.

He smiled.

Her grin stretched all the way across her face. She could feel it. And then he was through his fellow passengers, in front of her, and she was in his arms.

Holding on as if she'd never let go.

Because she never was going to let go of him again. This time, no matter what, her big brother was in her life to stay.

THE WOMAN WASN'T home. In black jeans and a clean gray T-shirt, Chris stood at her front door in flip-flops, having knocked three times, and accepted the fact that this wasn't going to be over as soon as he'd determined it would be. He wanted to see her, then get the hell out of the middle-class, suburban part of town.

It had to be clear to everyone who passed that he didn't belong there.

"Ms. Sanderson? I'm Detective Miller, come on in." At just under six feet, the man was shorter than she'd pictured. He made eye contact so briefly she wasn't sure it had happened, and then she was staring at his suited shoulders as he motioned toward a hallway with several doorways leading into rooms with large windows.

With the California rolls she and Cal had shared rumbling around in her stomach, she turned to look at the man who'd flown all the way from Tennessee to be with her. He nodded and, with a reassuring hand at her back, accompanied her down the hallway.

Miller led them to the last door on the left. Inside, a young, blonde woman sat on the far side of a conference table. She stood as they entered.

"Ms. Sanderson, this is Detective Lucy Hayes. I hope you don't mind if she sits in with us."

The other detective Cal had told her about.

Shaking her head, Emma smiled at Detective Hayes, taking the hand she offered. Detective Hayes might be a small woman, a couple of inches shorter than Emma's five and a half feet, but there was nothing weak about her grip.

"Detective Hayes has been working with

me on this case," Miller said. "She's helping me on her own time, not as an official member of my team. I just need to make that clear."

"The detective from Aurora," Cal said, his eyes narrowing in a way Emma already recognized as his quietly assessing look.

Miller eyed Emma's brother. "Sorry," she said, so focused on breathing that she'd forgotten her manners. "Detective Miller, this is Caleb Whittier. I understand you two have met by phone several times."

"Mr. Whittier." Miller stepped forward and shook Cal's hand. "Good to meet you in person."

"Good to meet you, too," Cal said. Then he peered over at the female detective. "Since you're so far from home, are we to assume that you found something to do with our case?"

Fear gripped Emma as the two detectives exchanged a glance. After twenty-five years of needing to know, she wasn't ready.

"What?" Emma asked when the silence became unbearable. Miller nodded at Hayes.

"It's probably nothing." Lucy Hayes looked Emma right in the eye. "I'm actually working on a different case, also a baby abduction, that took place around the same time your sister went missing. I signed out the evidence kit for my case and it turned out to contain some evidence that fit Peter Walters's M.O."

"The pervert you told me about," Emma said, looking at Detective Miller. His suit was green. Hunter green. A suit. Not slacks and a jacket. The tie had thin, dark green stripes set amid beige and brown.

Her baby sister had not been molested at two years of age. The knowledge would kill Rose.

Her throat closed up. Her lips started to tremble. She bit them from the inside.

"That's right," Miller said.

"Did you tie that case to him?" Cal asked what Emma could not.

"Fortunately, no," Lucy Hayes replied evenly. "But there's a minor similarity between the case I'm working on in Aurora and a piece of information from Cal's book that Detective Miller told me about. We're checking on it but haven't turned up anything substantial yet." Her smile, given mostly to Emma, was soft. Warm. "I had vacation coming so I took this week off to be here and follow up with Ramsey. Ramsey told me about meeting with you and I wanted to meet you both. I also wanted to ask your permission to take a sample of Claire's DNA back to Indiana with me. I have a private lab in Cincinnati that is doing some work for me on the cold-case abductions I'm looking at there."

Nodding, Emma relaxed a notch. She didn't have to accept anything just yet. "Okay. If it will help."

The detectives exchanged another glance and Lucy gave a short nod.

"Lucy has been working on her original case a long time," Miller told Cal and Emma. "She has a lot of information at her disposal. Some pretty impressive databases she's set up on her own dime. It's not just a job to her. If there's something to find she'll find it."

Cal's hand settled in the middle of Emma's back.

It was time. Emma slid her hand inside her bag. She didn't have to look to find what she was after. She knew right where it was. Pulling out the box, she extended her arm toward the detectives.

The detectives asked Emma and Cal to talk about the day Claire went missing.

Lucy Hayes wrapped her hand around Emma's. "We'll take care of it for you." Her softly spoken words referred to the box. Emma was turning over so much more.

She clung to it, finally giving in to the gentle tug of the female detective's hand.

"If you're up to it, we have some questions for you," Ramsey Miller said.

Emma glanced at the little wooden box of ribbons in Lucy's hands, then at Cal. "Okay," she said, and the two of them took seats opposite the detectives.

The detectives asked Emma and Cal to talk about the day Claire went missing.

Together, they recounted the story of that day. Their memories sometimes gelled and sometimes collided as the detectives recorded the conversation.

Emma and Cal both remembered their regular babysitter being sick that day. And Rose, on the phone making arrangements and then telling them that she'd have to pick them up after school.

They both remembered Claire's bear at the breakfast table. Cal thought she'd been in her high chair. Emma remembered her sister kneeling in a big-people chair.

Cal remembered that Claire climbed like a monkey and that was why she was still in a high chair and not a booster seat.

Emma remembered the climbing, too, but couldn't remember why her sister didn't have a booster seat.

They both remembered the detective later finding Claire's teddy bear in Cal's father's car.

Emma thought Cal's father had been in the house for a long time after breakfast. Cal had been the first to leave.

They both remembered the truck that delivered meat in the neighborhood, but only Cal remembered seeing it that day.

Neither of them saw anyone else.

The whole time they talked, Emma watched the detectives, wondering what Detective Hayes had found in Cal's book. She assumed the detectives couldn't say because it had to do with another case, as well, and she wasn't as upset about that as she might have been.

She just wasn't ready.

"And who, in your current lives, knows any of these details?" Miller asked when, more than an hour later, they'd run out of things to say.

"My fiancée, Morgan Lowen, knows most of them," Cal said.

"Her knowledge is recent, right?" Miller asked, his gaze intense. "Since the box of evidence disappeared."

"Right."

"And how about you?" Detective Hayes appeared equally serious as she questioned Emma.

"I rarely talk about the past," Emma said. "I mean, everyone knows about Claire—my mother and I do a lot of local campaigning for child-safety awareness—but we don't discuss details."

"How about other family members?"

"My family is just my mother and me and my grandfather in Florida. Mom, by the way, knows nothing about this meeting. Or about…Peter Walters…or any investigation. My mother's…fragile…where Claire is concerned."

Both detectives nodded. "Detective Miller told me you'd asked to leave your mother out of this for now," Hayes said, and then asked, "have you ever been married?"

"No."

"What about love interests? Is there anyone in your life that you might have confided in?"

Her face hot, Emma experienced a flash of humiliation as she thought of Chris. Were they watching her? Could they know?

But she hadn't confided in Chris. So he was a moot point.

"I…was engaged," she said, refocusing her thoughts. "To Rob Evert." Another humiliating episode she'd rather not talk about, but preferable to the lobsterman debacle. "He knows about Claire, of course. He knows about this meeting, too, actually." She glanced at Cal. She'd told him of her bro-

ken engagement. "Rob's been very supportive, helping my mother and me with various
fund-raisers, and so on. He knows all about
our efforts to find Claire. But he never asked
about the day she went missing. He understood that it's a painful memory. And…like
I said, I don't talk about it. It's not like I remember all that much from before the abduction, anyway. Or—" she paused, shared
a look with Cal "—I didn't realize how much
I remembered until Cal and I started talking
about it. I was only four. And until Claire
was…gone…it was just an ordinary day."

She remembered that night, though. The
long hours when no one went to bed and she
was afraid to go to sleep. To leave her mother's side at all. And she remembered the horrible, nightmarish days that followed, too.
Her mother never smiled or laughed in those
days. She was never in a good mood after
that.

And Emma was never unafraid.

She'd lost her baby sister—and her childhood, too.

CHAPTER FOURTEEN

FOR ALL CHRIS KNEW Emma Sanderson worked second shift. Or nights. Or didn't work at all. Her name and address were all his called-in favor had netted.

Sitting in his shiny black pickup across the street from her house Monday night, he wondered if ten o'clock was too late to pay her a visit.

He'd just pulled up and a light was still on behind the big front window. One she left on when she was away? Did she even live alone?

He'd been by three times. The light had been on two of those three times. He didn't relish the idea of making the half-hour trip back over here anytime soon. And he didn't want a repeat of the previous sleepless night, either. Better just to get it over with.

While he was sitting there, debating what to do, a blue car pulled into Emma's drive. The garage door opened and the car pulled in, the door closing behind it even before the engine had stopped.

Chris had failed to notice if she'd been alone.

Still, there was no decision to make here.

THE KNOCK ON her door startled Emma, stimulating a rush of adrenaline, followed by dread.

Rob.

He knew how she felt about answering the door at night.

Rob was intimately acquainted with the fears she battled every day of her life. Fears that her mother had implanted in her at a very young age, telling her that those fears would keep her safe.

His antics were escalating if he was trying to scare her into believing she needed him.

Going to the door, Emma grabbed the handle with one hand, the dead bolt with the other, ready to undo the latter and pull on the former. At the last second, she put one eye to the peephole that had been installed at exactly her height.

And fear of a new breed took root inside her. It wasn't Rob at the door.

But it was a man she had to deal with once and for all.

"Chris?" she said as she opened the heavy wooden door just enough to speak to him, leaving the screen door firmly closed.

"Yeah. I'd have called but I don't know your number."

"How did you know my address?" Was he more of a creep than she had thought? Had he been following her?

It was a ridiculous thought. She'd spent the night with the man in the most intimate way possible. She knew he wasn't a creep.

Just a fisherman who lived a lifestyle so far removed from hers that she couldn't understand it at all.

How could a man put his job above his family? Above a wife and children? It wasn't as if the ocean would take care of him in his old age.

"I know some cops," Chris said. "Saved me from having to hire a private detective."

His words didn't help the tension holding her rigid. "You had me investigated?"

But if he knew cops, he couldn't be all bad. Unless they were...

"Nope. They ran a check on your license plate and gave me your last name and address. If you sue them for it, you'll win. They trusted that you'd want to see me."

He'd made an effort to find her. He'd have called if she'd left her phone number for him.

Emma's heart fluttered. And her lower region started to dance.

"What did you want to talk about?" Emma leaned against the door, clinging to it, exhausted from a day spent dealing with myriad emotions. And she found herself liking Chris anew.

Because he'd tried to contact her, after all.

"I'd...kind of like to come in to discuss it, if I may."

If he was going to kill her, he'd had plenty of opportunity a few weeks ago when he'd had her alone and naked in his hotel room.

"I had a rough day," she blurted. To explain whatever she might do next? Put him off? Send him away?

"This won't take long."

Nodding, Emma unlocked the screen door, and stood back, letting him into her foyer. She led the way into the living room. The couches were brown leather—chosen with Rob in mind. So was the recliner.

Her hand-carved rocking chair was adorned with a brightly colored quilt she'd made during her senior year of high school. With her mother's blessing she'd used fabric from some of Claire's old clothes.

Tonight, she headed straight for security, settling into the chair and pulling the quilt onto her lap.

Chris, a very different-looking Chris than the one she'd made love with, settled back onto the couch with the ease of a man who planned to stay awhile. Or who had the ability to make himself comfortable wherever he happened to be. She'd always admired that trait.

"What did you want to talk about?" Had he seen her at the dock? Was that when he'd seen her license plate?

Cody had probably told him she'd been to Citadel's, too.

How embarrassing. The man probably thought *she* was stalking *him*.

With a sick feeling, she realized he probably hadn't been looking for her because the night they'd shared had meant as much to him as it had to her. He'd come to let her down gently. To ask that she quit following him.

"What was so rough about your day?" His voice was quiet and deep, laced with indiscernible emotion.

Not trusting her composure, she shook her head.

"Were you at work?"

"No. I was at the police station." The words sounded factual. Unemotional.

"The police station? Are you in some kind of trouble?"

He could have sounded put off. Horrified. He didn't. Which was comforting.

But, then, he came from a rough part of town.

"Do you need help?"

How could she still be affected by that voice, those eyes, after what she knew of him? After he'd left her alone in that hotel room with no way to connect again?

Emma's lips started to tremble. She thought of her students. Her classroom. She took a deep breath—assuming the authority figure—and proceeded to give him an abbreviated version of her day.

"Your sister was abducted and no one ever found her?"

"Mmm-hmm." She never got used to the shocked reaction.

"I'd go nuts."

Momentarily disarmed by his matter-of-fact tone, she paused, and then said, "Yeah, I do." He'd nailed it completely. When the pain became more than she could bear, she went nuts. Drove herself nuts. Drove anyone around her nuts.

Just like Rose did.

"How long until you find out the DNA results?"

"I'm not sure. A week or two. The Comfort Cove DNA lab is small so they're sending it to Boston, but they take current cases first."

She had no real idea how long it would take.

"That's crap. To make you wait."

She shrugged, and started to rock slowly and steadily. "I've been waiting twenty-five years. I'd rather they use their resources to try and prevent current crimes first."

"It's going to be hard. Knowing."

"If this guy's the one, yeah."

"As hard as the not knowing is, there's comfort in the chance she'll show up someday."

Hugging her quilt, Emma tilted her head and smiled. "You know someone who's gone through this?"

"Hell, no!" His smile was empathetic. "Just seems obvious—the knowing and not knowing would both be hard.…"

"You know what's crazy?" she asked. "Tonight while I was sitting there, I realized that somewhere along the way, not knowing became safe. I know I can deal with not knowing. I know *how* to deal with it."

"Why is that crazy?"

"Because from the time I was four years old, the main priority in our lives has been to find Claire. At whatever cost."

"Your reaction doesn't make you crazy." Chris's gaze was warm, but there was no pity in it. "It makes you normal. Change is hard," he said, "even when it's good change. It's normal to resist."

Emma offered him a glass of tea. He accepted. And somehow an hour passed as she told Chris about Cal Whittier, too.

But he still hadn't told her anything about himself.

"What do you do for a living?" he asked, cradling his nearly empty glass of tea in his hands.

"I teach American History."

He quirked one eyebrow. "Really? What level?"

"High school. All four grades."

"I quit school before I graduated." His admission surprised her. He didn't seem the type to have quit school.

"Where did you learn to play the piano?"

"Home. My grandmother had a piano. I'm self-taught. I play by ear." He had enormous room for ego. Yet he spoke as though he'd just told her he'd taught himself to make grilled cheese.

She complimented him on his talent.

And then there was silence.

It was after eleven and she had to teach in the morning.

"You said you had something to talk to me about." A brush-off wouldn't be fun, but if it was coming, she might as well get it over with.

In fact a brush-off would be good. It would be easier than having to tell her piano man there was no way she could get involved with a lobsterman. Ever.

"I have a question to ask." His hesitance set her heart racing again.

He was going to ask her out.

He couldn't.

She'd have to tell him no.

She didn't want to. She wanted to be loved by a man who loved her so much that that love changed him.

Her journal was in the drawer less than three feet away from Chris. He didn't need to be changed. He was perfect as he was.

Just not for her.

He was a man of the sea.

She had to be brave.

"You said you had a question to ask?"

"Did I get you pregnant?"

CHAPTER FIFTEEN

"WHAT?"

A little taken aback by Emma's reaction, Chris repeated his question. "I asked you if you're pregnant."

"No! Of course I'm not!"

Her conviction was good, but his gut wasn't satisfied.

"You're on the pill, then?"

"No."

"Have you had a period?"

Emma stared at him openmouthed, and then said, "I don't think that's any of your business."

"I disagree. Considering the circumstances, it's my business as much as it is yours." He'd apologize for his harshness later. Maybe. Right now they had to get this done.

"The circumstances?"

Damn him for remembering what those arms, currently strangling that blanket, had felt like wrapped around his neck. His waist. His legs.

Damn him.

"We had sex two weeks and three days ago. I ejaculated inside of you. Twice."

And, Lord help him, he wanted to be inside her again. Right then. Right there.

He watched the expressions chase themselves across her face. Horror. Fear. Discomfort. And something else. Something that reminded him of that night at Citadel's when her eyes had met his across the room.

What in the hell was the matter with him?

He was petrified of letting this woman ruin his life and he wanted her again, too.

"You wore a condom." Her voice broke on the last word.

"They're only good for one go."

Watching Emma suck in her lower lip, as though she was biting it from the inside, Chris felt her pain. He'd been drunk and high on her, and an absolute ass.

Emma stood, leaving the chair rocking at full force. "I am not pregnant. Rest assured I am absolutely certain of that fact." Standing in the archway, her back to the foyer, she watched him, as though waiting for him to leave.

"You've had a period, then?"

He had to hand it to her, she didn't lower her gaze. She flinched, but she didn't look away.

"No."

"So you don't know for certain that you aren't pregnant."

"I do know."

"How?"

"Because I know my body. I'd know if I was pregnant. There'd be…changes."

"When were you due?" His mom and dad might have up and died on him, but they'd taught him a thing or two besides how to fish before they left him. Such as how to clean the toilet bowl. Wash darks with darks and lights with lights. Make an omelet. And the basics of a woman's cycle.

"I'm irregular."

Not the free pass he was looking for.

"There's only one other option, then."

"What?"

"You have to take a pregnancy test."

"I—"

"We can go right now and pick one up. They're only a few bucks and available in any all-night drugstore. You pee on a strip and in a few minutes we'll know."

She took a big breath, but he didn't get to hear what she'd been about to say because she started to choke. Tears came to her eyes.

Chris went to the kitchen, found a glass, filled it with water and carried it in to her.

He couldn't be a father. He couldn't go out on the ocean knowing that he was leaving behind someone whose life depended on him. And he couldn't not go out on the ocean. He'd rather be dead. He'd tried to explain his feelings to Sara and the honesty had netted him a broken engagement.

By the time he returned to the living room, Emma had quieted and took the glass, swallowing half of the liquid without a word.

"I know what a pregnancy test is, Chris," she said, sounding the calmest she had since he'd arrived.

He wanted to ask if she'd taken one before, but forced himself to stay focused on the present. Her past—her future—were none of his concern.

Until he confirmed that he was not about to be a daddy.

He stood and yanked his keys out of the front pocket of his jeans. "Then let's go."

She stood, too, but shook her head.

"I can't accept a 'no,' Emma," he said, trying to be firm, but starting to panic. Some men could fish five days a week and go home and be with their families. Some men could put family first. Chris's father hadn't been one of them. And neither was Chris.

His mother had suffered. Ultimately, everyone had suffered.

"I need to know if there are consequences from our night together." He tried to speak calmly. "I know we're talking about your body at the moment, but if we created...if you're pregnant, then our lives are equally changed. I have to know."

Her dark eyes took on that glow again, or the simmer or whatever the hell it was that they did that messed him up inside and made him do things that were completely out of character. Like reach for her hand. Bring it to his lips. Kiss the palm.

And meet her gaze. He stopped short of promising her he'd do whatever she wanted him to do. But only barely.

"Please," he said.

Leaving her hand in his, she said, "I understand. And...you're not being unfair. I just can't do it tonight. Meeting Cal...taking in those ribbons...my mom... I just... I'm on emotional overload. I can't take the tension of waiting for an answer tonight. I guess this doesn't make any sense." Her expression pleaded with him. "I know I'm not pregnant, so there shouldn't be any tension, but—"

"How about tomorrow?" he asked. It was

late. They were both tired. News sat better on rested souls. "I can pick up the test and meet you here around six."

"Okay."

He stepped closer and took her other hand. "Don't cry."

"I'm not going to." But she was. He could see the moisture gathering in her eyes.

"I didn't mean to upset you."

"You didn't. It's not you. It's just…everything is closing in on me. But I'm strong and I can handle it. I'm a survivor."

Her chin trembled. And her gaze didn't drop at all as tears spilled from her eyes and down her cheeks.

Just as openly as she'd given him her passion, she gave him raw emotion.

And Chris did what he had to do. He took her into his arms, sat down with her and held her.

She didn't say a word. Eventually her breathing evened and Chris realized she'd fallen asleep. He thought about ways to put her down easily. To slide out from beneath her. He considered carrying her upstairs. It shouldn't be too hard to find a bed to place her in up there.

Feeling more relaxed than he had in weeks, he ran through his options. He slid down to a more comfortable position while he decided what to do.

At some point, all those sleepless nights caught up with him.

EMMA WOKE UP slowly. She was usually an easy riser, a person who didn't lollygag around in bed, who got right up, but today she didn't want to give up the coziness of sleep.

Since when was sleep cozy for her?

A heart was beating beneath her cheek. Suddenly, she was wide-awake, listening to the even breathing of a man she'd slept with but never seen asleep.

Dawn was just creeping in through the living-room curtains, making it between five and six in the morning. She had to be in the shower by six-thirty. She had to take a pregnancy test less than twelve hours after that.

Weird how, lying there on the couch against the warmth of Chris's chest, the idea didn't seem so completely alarming. She really didn't think she was pregnant. And imagining Chris with her, maybe even holding her hand, while they waited for the results that would reassure him, made the activity seem less like an ordeal and more of an inconvenience that she could handle.

When she was pretty certain she was out of time, she carefully disentangled herself from him, covered him with the quilt made from Claire's clothes and quietly climbed the stairs.

Back in the living room half an hour later she wrote a note, telling Chris to lock up after himself, folded it as he'd folded the one he'd left for her in the hotel room and propped it on the table beside the couch.

She left the house with a smile on her face.

CHRIS GOT TO work late. Very late. If he hadn't had to pull Trick's traps, too, he might not have gone out at all. He hadn't slept so many hours in a row since puberty.

Late to work meant late coming in. He'd hoped to finish installing the engine in his boat that night and be driving her by Wednesday—and he could have, if he hadn't had to be all the way on the other side of Comfort Cove by six. He had no way of contacting Emma Sanderson.

She still hadn't given him her cell-phone number.

Damn. He'd spent the night with her twice now, but he still didn't know her number.

He'd hoped to have time to shower after work. He didn't even get a chance to stop at home. Changing into an old, ripped pair of jeans and a gray T-shirt he had stored on the *Son Catcher,* he exchanged his deck shoes for flip-flops and jogged toward the truck.

The woman was messing up his life. He had to be done with her.

CHAPTER SIXTEEN

"RELAX, IT'S GOING to be fine." Emma smiled at Chris in her office, across the hall from the bathroom where, the little test strip was processing.

"You're obviously not opposed to having a family," he said, frowning down at his flip-flops.

The man had nice toes. Well shaped. Perfectly sized for his feet. Tan.

"I hope to have a family someday. But only after I'm married to the man I want to spend the rest of my life with."

She could *not* have the baby of a fisherman.

"How long has it been?"

Perched on a desk chair, she glanced at the large round watch on her wrist—a gift from the parents of her graduating students the previous year. "Two minutes. Three more to go."

He leaned against the edge of her desk, his hands braced on either side of him. "I'm never going to marry," he said. "It wouldn't be right knowing that I can't give a family the priority it deserves. I'm like my father— I belong on the water."

She knew all about the lobstering life from Rose.

"How long have you been lobstering?"

"All my life. My father was out on the *Son Catcher*—that's my boat—the day I was born."

Any minute hope she'd harbored that he was just trying out the life, that he'd leave it someday, went out the window.

Their fathers had both been fishermen. And it sounded as if they'd both placed the sea above their own families. An omen.

"Do you fish year-round?"

"Yeah. Some states don't allow it. Massachusetts does."

"I hear it's dangerous."

He shrugged. "Living is dangerous. I know what I'm doing. And if it's my time, it's my time."

Two minutes left.

With his head still bent, he glanced at her. "You ever been out on a fishing boat?"

"No."

She'd never even been down to the docks until two days ago.

"It's indescribable out there." His voice took on a new note, filled with some of the same emotion she'd pulled from his music. "The vastness, the freedom, the quiet—it's addictive. The solitude is hard for some people—I thrive on it. And the waves...every day it's something new. Every day they ask me if I'm up to the challenge and I know that the day I'm not is the day I die."

"Do you live on your boat?"

"Not technically, no. It has a small galley. I spend the occasional night out on the water."

"And the rest of the time?"

He shook his head. Glanced at her watch. "I live in a small place not far from the docks."

She nodded. A minute and a half to go.

"Does your dad still fish with you?"

"My folks are both gone." He looked up. "They passed away nearly ten years ago. In a freeway pile-up not fifteen minutes from here."

"They were together?"

He nodded.

"I'm so sorry."

"Me, too."

The pause between them could have been awkward, but it wasn't. She wanted to put her arms around him and hold him like he'd held her the night before.

"Do you have siblings?"

"No." And then in the same breath, he said, "How much longer?"

"One minute."

And as soon as he saw that the test was negative, he'd be gone from her life.

CHRIS FOLLOWED EMMA into her bathroom. He had to know he was okay.

He had to know that she was going to be fine, too. Unencumbered, as she sought answers regarding her sister.

Holding his breath, he waited as she picked up the strip from the edge of the sink.

She looked at it and didn't say anything.

"Well?" He glanced over her shoulder, and had no idea what he was looking at. What the colors meant.

With the stick in one hand, Emma picked up the folded instructions.

That couldn't be good.

"What is it?"

The sense of dread that descended on him weighed more than a full lobster trap coming up from the bottom of the ocean.

"It's inconclusive," she said, staring at the device.

"What does that mean?"

"I'm not sure."

"You're pregnant."

"It's not a positive result."

"So, you're not pregnant."

"It's not a negative result, either," Emma said on her way back to the office. Placing the stick carefully on top of the instructions, she sat down at her desk, and called up an internet browser on her computer. While Chris's life started to unravel, she typed in, "Pregnancy test inconclusive."

He was wearing a T-shirt. In September. And sweating profusely. Envisioning a kid in his parents' house.

Where? His parents' room hadn't been touched since the day they'd been killed. The wood floors in the house needed refinishing. There were splinters where the washer had overflowed into the kitchen a few years back.

He was never there. He couldn't have a kid at his home.

A vision formed in his mind. Eyes—brown eyes like Emma's—staring at him accusingly. Disappointment there. All the things he'd felt toward his father during his growing-up years—until he was old enough to join the old man on the boat.

Then he saw his mother's eyes. Directed

at him. She'd forbidden him to leave her as his father had. Later, she'd begged. For Sara's sake.

He turned, faced the door. The air was stifling.

"It means there's an elevated amount of human chorionic gonadotropin in my system."

"What the hell is that?"

"A hormone that's present in a woman's body during pregnancy."

He knew it. God help him.

"The test was positive?"

"No, there wasn't enough HCG to indicate pregnancy." The tranquility in Emma's eyes calmed him. "Look, Chris. It says here that the levels could be higher right before my cycle. I'm probably going to have a period soon."

"So that's it? We just wait? For how long? You said you were irregular. When will we know?"

He needed a drink. On the deck of the *Son Catcher.* Far out in the water. He wasn't in control out there, either, but at least on the ocean he understood the rules.

"It recommends waiting a week and retesting. It also recommends a blood test. I'll call my doctor in the morning."

He didn't feel a damn bit better. "Have you ever thought you were pregnant before?"

"No. Except for that one night with you, I've always been extremely careful."

"But you aren't on the pill."

"There's a history of blood clots in my family. The pill increases the risk, so my doctor wouldn't prescribe it for me. I wouldn't have taken it even if she had—not with the risk."

Emma turned off her computer and headed for the door. He followed her back downstairs. He should go. He could still get some work done on the boat by spotlight.

In the living room, he saw the couch where he'd spent the night. A surprisingly restful night.

And he wondered why there wasn't a man, sharing it with her. It didn't make much sense. Emma was in a class all her own. Her beauty and body aside, she exuded everything good that was female.

"You've got a white band of skin on your ring finger." Like some kind of idiot, he stood in the middle of her living room, not leaving.

"A broken engagement."

"Your idea, or his?"

"Mine."

He nodded. Like Sara. "Lucky you got out before it was too late."

"I'm not so sure I did. We were together for five years."

He folded his arms across his chest. "Did you love him?"

"I thought I did. I loved the life he represented."

"What made you change your mind?"

"More like 'who.'" She stood opposite him, her arms crossed, too. "More than one *who*."

"He cheated on you?"

"Several times. But that was before we got engaged."

"You knew he'd been unfaithful to you and you agreed to marry him, anyway?"

Shrugging, she said, "Like I said, I wanted the life he promised me."

"You wanted to be with a man who slept with other women?"

"I wanted to be with Rob because he knows me. He knows my mother. He not only understood that our lives revolve around finding Claire, he took on the quest to find her, too. And…he was okay with pandering to my mother's idiosyncrasies. And I truly believed, because he promised, that after we were engaged there would be no more fooling around."

"But there was."

"Yes."

"Recently?"

"I found him in bed with someone, just before I went to Citadel's that night. I gave him the night to get his stuff and get out."

Enlightenment. "Were you planning to stay in the tourist district that night?"

"For the first time in my life I had no plans. And look where it got me."

He tried not to take that personally, considering why they were together that evening. But he couldn't stop himself.

"As I recall, you rather...enjoyed...yourself that night. I remember you saying something about never having had an orgasm before?" His body reacted to the memory. Or to the words. Or to her.

He had a boat to fix.

A life to live.

She blushed. "I said that out loud?"

"You don't remember?"

"I remember thinking it."

"You want to think it again?" He didn't just say that.

"I...I mean, I can't, really, can I, since I... have...had, you know, one."

The woman entranced him. It had to be her

youth, was all. He was getting old. Jaded. Used to the company of more weathered women.

"You want to feel it again?"

"Of course I do! Now that I know what… Well, clearly Rob wasn't the right man. Next time I'll know not to settle for… I'm sure I'll find the right man and when I do—"

"I meant now. Tonight. With me."

"With you?"

"It's not like we haven't done it before. Or like either one of us is likely to be doing it with anyone else until we know for sure that we didn't create a baby together."

He was a heel. Using the pregnancy she was sure didn't exist to get her back in the sack. He'd never sunk so low. What in the hell was the matter with him?

He'd blame it on the beer.

But there hadn't been any.

He was stone-cold sober.

And hard as stone, too.

So he said, just to be clear, "I would very much like, with your permission, to make love with you again. Tonight."

CHAPTER SEVENTEEN

EMMA BURNED FROM the inside out. Her skin felt hot. Beneath her skin was hot. She was hot in private places that nice girls didn't share with many people.

"You have my permission," she choked out. She wasn't drunk. Or being pressured.

She wanted to have sex with Chris Talbot. Needed to feel the exquisite sensation again.

Without Chris, her life was all about hurt. And worrying about more hurt. Hers. Her mother's. Her sweet baby sister's.

God help her, Chris took the hurt away.

He moved. She saw the T-shirt and torn jeans. The flip-flops. His toes. And remembered the office upstairs, the reason he was there.

"Wait." She didn't step back when his chest touched her breasts.

His hands remained at his sides. "What?"

"Do you have a condom?" Rob had taken their supply.

"In my wallet." They were nose to nose, so close she could feel the movement of his lips.

Then their lips were touching. Emma opened her mouth, melted her tongue against his and prayed that her mother would forgive her for having sex with a man from the docks.

CHRIS HAD ALWAYS gotten up after sex. Sara had been the only woman to complain about it, but he figured there'd been others who would've preferred he lie with them for a while.

He just couldn't seem to make himself do it. Once it was over, he was done.

And he told himself to get his naked ass up from the bed of clothes they'd made on Emma's couch. He had a long drive ahead and an early morning. There was no reason to linger.

With one palm, he cupped her belly. "It's so flat." Strangely, the idea of his baby growing there didn't bring forth the usual panic. He felt too good to feel bad at the moment, he supposed.

Or maybe he was too weak to muster the energy. Probably why he was still lying there, cradling her naked body half on top of his.

"You don't have to worry, Chris."

"I wish I was as certain of that."

"Trust me, if I thought, for one second, that I was carrying a child, I'd be the first one to panic. An unplanned pregnancy would be disastrous for me, but to be pregnant with a fisherman's baby? I can't think of much worse."

Not sure what to say to that, Chris lay there, his hand stilled. "Mind explaining that?" he finally offered.

She leaned up on one elbow, studying his expression. Her eyes shadowed. "I'm so sorry," she said, frowning. "I just realized how that sounded."

He was still waiting for an explanation.

"You said your father was a fisherman," she said.

"That's right."

"And yet, you don't think you can be a father because you fish."

"I'm old-fashioned enough, hell, just plain old enough, to believe that a man and a woman should be married to have children," he said.

"I'm with you on that. Completely."

"The life of a fisherman does not lend itself to healthy marriages. Some people make it work. A lot don't. In my experience, most don't. So many times they live separate lives in the same house. I wouldn't be good with that kind of relationship."

Marta and Jim were the exception. Somehow they'd managed.

And Trick and his wife.

There were a few others he knew of.

"Is that what happened with your parents?"

"You could say that."

"I'm asking you what you say to that."

She was asking him to tell her things he didn't talk about. Not even to Sara.

"I was twelve when I caught my mother in bed with another man."

He made himself look her in the eyes, compelling brown eyes that turned compassionate.

"It wasn't the first time it had happened."

"Did your father know?"

"Eventually. I'm not sure when he found out. Or how. Nothing was ever said to me about it."

"Did he divorce her?"

"No, he pretended he didn't know. As near as I could tell, he felt responsible, which is crazy if you ask me. Yeah, he left her alone, all day every day for weeks and weeks at a time. But it was a flaw in her character that allowed her to give herself over to the arms of another man. At least while she was still married. She'd made vows to my dad."

"It couldn't have been easy. Growing up knowing that about your mom. But it must have been hard for her, too. Did she and your dad do things together when he wasn't fishing?"

"By the time he got home at night, he was exhausted. And every single time he went out on the boat, not only was he unavailable in case of an emergency, but he was also putting himself in danger. She'd worry, every day, that this would be the day she'd get the call. Even when the sun was shining and the waves were kind. When she got to the point where she couldn't stand it, he promised her he'd cut back, that he'd be home more, fish fewer days. But every morning, when he woke up, he'd hear the call and off he'd go.

"I'm not saying the blame was all Mom's. She was sensitive. And emotional. She needed a man around her to feel safe."

"He left even knowing that she was turning to other men?"

"Yeah."

"Maybe he just didn't love her enough."

"The one and only instance I saw my father cry was one rare night we got home early—in time to see a truck pulling out of our driveway. I was about sixteen. I knew what was going on, but I hadn't known that he did. He asked me to get out of the truck, to tell my mother that he was going to buy cigarettes, and then he backed slowly down the drive. I saw the tears when he glanced up at the house."

"But he came back."

"As soon as he got the cigarettes he said he was going after. He came in the house, kissed my mother hello and asked what smelled so delicious. She'd had a casserole cooking in the oven for our dinner while she'd been having sex with another man."

Chris heard his voice. Recognized it. But nothing else about himself was familiar at the moment. He'd taken complete and total leave of Chris Talbot.

"My father was a fisherman."

"What?" All his thoughts fled as he stared at her. "From Comfort Cove? Who is he? I must know him."

Good God, whose daughter had he just slept with?

"His name was Dale. Dale Sanderson. He was from around here, but he wasn't from a fishing family. He helped out at the docks for a couple of summers."

"Before you were born?"

"And after."

"So that would have been twenty-nine years ago," Chris said. "I was eleven and not really allowed down at the docks yet then, but Manny was there."

"From what I understand, my father worked on an older man's boat."

"Does you mother know about us?"

"Absolutely not! She'd be a wreck if she knew I'd been anywhere near the docks. I heard about the docks and the men who hung out there pretty much every time I went out from the time I hit puberty until I left for college. I wasn't supposed to drink or do drugs, but most especially I was not to venture anywhere near the docks. They aren't a safe place for girls."

"I agree with your mother." Honor forced him to speak up. He wasn't good for her. Not in the long-term.

Emma laid her head against his chest. "Mom's understandably neurotic," she said, "but she's also right a lot of the time. My father married her when she was pregnant with me. And then, when she got pregnant with Claire, he was offered a job in Alaska, working at sea full-time, with the promise of his own boat after a couple of years."

"Your mother didn't want to live in Alaska

all alone." He knew the drill. Understood. Sara couldn't stand the thought of living in Comfort Cove, the town where she grew up, where her family and most of her friends still lived, all alone. She hadn't wanted sole responsibility of raising their children.

"He didn't want to take us. He filed for divorce and took off."

"He paid child support, though, right?" The near darkness of the room held them in a cocoon that was apart from real life.

"No."

"Have you ever heard from him? Did he get his boat?" And was the boat worth sacrificing his family for?

Chris was afraid he knew the answer to that one.

"He didn't live long enough."

"What happened?"

"The classic bad-boy story," Emma said, her tone dry. "Shortly after arriving in Alaska, he got involved with a married woman and her husband came looking for my father. He found him drunk in a bar. There was a fight. My father ended up unconscious and later died. He'd still had my mother listed as next of kin on his life-insurance policy."

"So your mother got support money in a roundabout way."

"The payout was barely enough to cover the cost of the funeral."

"What about his parents? Did you know your grandparents?"

"I don't know anything about them. He was in foster care from a pretty young age, which is how he ended up in Comfort Cove."

"What about your mother? Do you have grandparents nearby?"

"No. They disowned her when she turned up pregnant with me, but they came around after I was born. We lived with them after my father left until Claire was born, but I don't remember that time. Mom had her teaching degree by then and had met Frank, whom they loved. But after Claire was taken...everything just went crazy, you know? Mom shut everyone out. My grandmother fell apart. She couldn't do anything. She cried any time she saw either one of us. Eventually she and my grandfather moved to Florida. My grandmother died a couple of years ago."

And he thought he'd had a hard life. Emma Sanderson was stronger than he'd ever had a hope of being.

"What happened to him?"

"He's still down there, living in the retirement community they lived in together. He golfs all the time. Last year he married a widow he met at their resort. They came up for a couple of days over Christmas. Harriet's a decade younger than him and she adores him. I guess she had a rough first marriage. And no children, although she always wanted them. Anyway, I liked her. So did my mother."

She had family. Any child she had would have family.

And most clearly, he, a man of the sea, would not be welcome. He'd digest the knowledge later, when he wasn't feeling so complacent.

For now, he'd best take his freedom, and his pants, and get out.

CHAPTER EIGHTEEN

"MS. SANDERSON?"

Looking up from the tests she was grading after school on Friday, Emma put down her pen. "Tammy? Come on in."

The dark-haired sophomore came slowly forward. "There's a phone message for you in the office. I told Mrs. Olsen that I'd let you know."

Barbara Olsen, the high school's office administrator, had agreed to let Tammy spend the last period of the day volunteering in the office in place of attending a study hall the gifted student didn't need.

"Thanks, I'll stop in on my way out," she said, smiling, putting the rest of the papers in her leather briefcase and pulling on the black cardigan she'd worn with her black slacks and white blouse. "You aced your test."

"Oh, good!" The straight-A student seemed surprised every time she did well.

"How's your mother doing?"

Tammy stood just inside the doorway.

"Okay. She goes in for more treatments today. She really wants to be well and I know she'll make it."

Tammy's mother, a drug baby, had been fighting addiction problems since the day she was born. Usually she won the fight, but not always.

"You're staying with your aunt in the interim?"

"Yeah."

"Is your uncle in town?" The man scared Tammy, but he hadn't done anything overt enough to warrant contacting the authorities. And staying with her aunt kept Tammy out of the child-welfare system and foster care.

"Not right now. He gets back next week."

"How long is your mother going to be away for this time?"

"Six weeks."

Most of the fall semester.

"You've got my number programmed into your cell phone, right?"

"Yes, ma'am."

"Do not hesitate to use it, Tammy. For any reason. If you just miss your mom and want to talk, you call me."

"Yes, ma'am."

"I mean it, Tammy," Emma spoke firmly. "I promised your mother I would be here for you when she couldn't be. That's how the world works. She got dealt some hard cards, and because of that, so did you. But you were also dealt a lot of good cards. I'm one of your aces, okay?"

With tears in her eyes, the girl nodded. "Thank you."

"Don't thank me. Just call me."

"I will."

Emma believed her.

THE PHONE MESSAGE was from Chris. She'd had sex with him twice now, but still had not exchanged phone numbers with him. He knew where she lived, where she worked— she'd told him the name of the school the night she'd told him what she did for a living. She knew where he worked. He thought they might be having a baby together…but they hadn't exchanged numbers. Or email addresses, either. He hadn't asked for hers. And she'd thought it for the best.

They had no future. There was no point in opening the means for convenient, immediate contact.

According to the note Barbara had left in her box, he'd not only asked her to call him, he'd said it was important. He'd left his number.

Walking out to her car, she punched the

digits into her list of contacts. She wasn't ready to speak to him yet. Perhaps it was the coward's way out, but she couldn't follow in her mother's footsteps and make the biggest mistake of her life. She couldn't let herself fall for a fisherman.

She had to let him know that her doctor was out of town until Monday of the following week and probably wouldn't be able to see her until Tuesday at the earliest, and that she wanted to wait to see her own physician.

He might not like that choice. But her body was hers and she was comfortable with her own doctor.

In spite of what Chris thought, there was no rush. Her doctor didn't even recommend a first prenatal exam until six weeks. And she couldn't let herself consider the *what ifs* of being pregnant. Not right now. She had so much coming at her and couldn't afford to let Chris's panic affect her. Anyway, they'd know soon enough.

Emma might be strong, but she was also smart enough to know that she couldn't afford another heartbreak. Not any time soon.

She'd just dropped her phone in her purse when the ring tone sounded. She didn't recognize the number, or even the area code.

Sitting in her car in the teachers' parking lot, she took the call.

"Hello?"

"Emma? This is Detective Lucy Hayes, you got a minute?"

She gulped. She wasn't ready. Not while facing a drive through town at dinnertime. Comfort Cove wasn't a metropolis, but it had more than doubled in size since she was a kid.

"I'm just leaving work...." The woman was a cop. Cops didn't encourage cell-phone distraction while operating a motor vehicle.

"I was wondering if we could meet," the detective said, her voice reassuringly calm.

"You have news."

"I have a couple of things to talk to you about. We can meet at the station," she said. "Miller's out on another case, but we can use his office. Or we can meet someplace less formal if you'd like. There's a coffeehouse not far from the station."

"The Caffeine Café," Emma said. "I go right by there on my way home."

"Do you have time to stop?"

She had all weekend. And she wasn't ready. "Of course. If I didn't have time, I would make time."

Claire came first. Always.

CHRIS STOPPED IN at Marta and Jim's after he left the docks Friday night.

"Well, it's about time you showed up for Friday-night dinner." Marta greeted him at the door, wiping her hands on her apron. "I've got fried tilapia and homemade chips nearly ready."

"I can't stay." He gave his automatic response to pretty much any invitation, and then said, "I just stopped by to let Jim know that Trick's going to be back on the water tomorrow. It would be good if he could keep an eye out for him."

"Come on in and tell him, then." Marta stood back, holding open the door leading into the kitchen, which looked the same as it had when he was a kid. "He's already at the table."

The room smelled just like he remembered Friday-night dinners smelling every week of his growing up.

"Sit down, boy," Jim said, nodding at the chair across from Marta's empty place.

Chris hesitated.

"He says he can't stay," Marta said, pulling a plate from the cupboard, silverware from the drawer, and shoving the drawer closed with her hip.

"Of course he can stay." The look he gave

Chris had Chris in his seat, a napkin spread across his lap, before Marta had the food on the table. There were some lessons a guy learned young and didn't have to learn twice.

Going against that look—the one his father and Jim had perfected—was one of those things.

Not getting a girl pregnant out of wedlock was another.

"You ever hear of a guy named Dale Sanderson?" Chris asked Jim a few minutes later, spearing a piece of fish with his fork.

Jim glanced up at him and away, frowning while he chewed. "Name rings a bell. Who's asking?"

"An old acquaintance of his was down at the docks a Sunday or two ago."

He wouldn't lie. But neither would he give them even a hint that he'd had a conversation with an unmarried female.

Heck, the first time he'd talked to Sara in school someone had told someone who told someone, and the next thing he knew his parents had heard about it. Then his mom told Marta, who told Jim, and the following Friday-night dinner the four of them had practically had him and Sara married.

The weeks after Sara had broken off their

engagement, the four of them had walked around looking as if someone had died.

But he wasn't just keeping quiet for himself. He was protecting Emma from any connection to the man she'd written off long ago.

Which didn't stop Chris from being curious.

He'd eaten several bites of tilapia before he realized that Jim hadn't said a word. Marta was frowning.

"So did you know him?" he asked, looking from one to the other.

"Heard of him," Jim said. "Seen him from afar. Never had occasion to speak with him."

"Sounds like you remember him well."

"He was a punk," Jim muttered. "Gave the docks, and those of us who worked hard for an honest living, a bad name."

"He was just a kid," Marta said.

"A punk kid." Jim, who was always kind, almost snorted on the last word.

"They said he stole from the boats," Marta put in.

"He hired on with Kennedy," Jim added, naming a man Chris could hardly remember, but one he'd heard a lot of stories about growing up. The man had been in his sixties when Chris was born, which would have made him close to seventy when Dale Sanderson worked for him.

Kennedy had never married. But he took at-risk boys from around town under his wing, taught them hard work and manners and honesty.

He'd died on his boat, out at sea. His traps had all been empty, his lobsters banded and ready to sell. It had appeared as if he'd just gone to sleep after a good day's work.

His will had stipulated that his boat, and everything else he owned, be sold and the money put into a scholarship fund at the local high school.

"Rumor was that Sanderson might have had something to do with Kennedy dying," Jim said, setting down his fork. "He'd married in between his first and second summers on the docks. Had a kid. Kennedy liked the girl—and took a shine to the baby, too. Then he found out that Sanderson had been stealing from him—taking the catch in to Manny every day and siphoning off the payout. He also found things missing from his house and the boat, too. When he confronted Sanderson, the guy laughed at him. Told him he was just an old dodder who should have quit years before. Said that Kennedy wouldn't be bringing in any fish at all if it weren't for

Dale. Claimed that the money was rightfully his since he did all the work…"

Chris was almost sorry he'd asked.

"Right about that time Dale found out that his wife was pregnant again," Marta said.

Chris took a bite of salad, glancing at her. "Did you know her? Sanderson's wife?"

"No." Marta shook her head. "She used to hang around down at the docks, that first summer, but she was just like any of the other high-school girls that think the fishing life is romantic, or the fisherman rugged because they're forbidden."

Marta had grown up down at the docks, the daughter of a fisherman. She'd known better.

"Once they were married, she never came down to the docks again."

"Sanderson wasn't the only one who behaved poorly," Jim said. "There's enough guys down at the dock who do exactly as outsiders claim they do—the drinking and fornicating and taking off from responsibility."

Chris knew all about them. To some men, fishing, being out on the ocean, was a way to escape from life's duties. The docks would always attract some of their kind.

"The young SOB got drunk and loud one night and told everyone down at the bar that

Kennedy wasn't up to fishing anymore, that he was a waste of weight on his own boat."

Oh, God, no. Chris felt the blow almost personally, figuring he knew exactly how that had to have felt to a man who'd given his entire life to the ocean.

"Next day, Kennedy took the boat out alone. Brought in his entire catch. Prepared 'em for sale. And died.

"By the time the dust settled after Kennedy's funeral, Sanderson had run off. I heard he divorced his wife while she was pregnant with their second baby.

"No one knows what happened to him, for sure," Jim said, picking up his fork again. "We were just glad to be rid of him."

Chris could have told the older man about Dale Sanderson's unfortunate fate. But it wasn't his story to tell.

And he didn't think he was going to tell Emma about the legacy she'd escaped, either. There was no point in her learning about a man she'd never known.

"THANKS FOR MEETING with me on such short notice." Detective Hayes, dressed in a fashionable tweed pant suit, met Emma at the door of the Caffeine Café.

"Of course." Emma pulled open the door

and held it for the detective. The woman walked into the place as if she owned it, in spite of being a few inches shorter than Emma. Her short blond hair bobbed as she moved.

Pulling her brown curls out from under the shoulder strap of her purse, Emma followed her inside.

They ordered coffee—black decaf for Emma, a caramel latte for Lucy—and found a small round table at the back of the room, across from a young man engrossed in his computer and wearing earbuds.

Lucy started in right away. "We got Claire's DNA results back today."

Holding her coffee cup between her hands, Emma soaked up the warmth. "So soon? I thought it would be a couple of weeks."

"So did Ramsey, but Shawn, at the lab, worked on the Walters case and he pushed it through. Ramsey was called out on a homicide just after Shawn called him, so I told him I'd meet with you. If that's all right with you?"

Emma nodded, just as happy to be dealing with Detective Hayes.

Staring down into the black liquid she'd yet to taste, Emma steeled herself. They'd been on this roller coaster for twenty-five years. It was time to get off.

She saw Lucy Hayes's fingers slide across the table just before the detective wrapped them around the top of Emma's hand where it still clutched her cup.

"There was no match between Claire's DNA and the Walters case."

Every muscle in her body gave way, leaving her weak. Limp. Relief was a physical ache as the tension she'd been holding in began to give up its grip.

When she could, she glanced up. "She wasn't one of his victims?"

Her blue eyes warm, Lucy shook her head. "None of the items found in Walters's basement link him to Claire."

"Thank God." Thank you, Lord. A thousand times, thank you. Emma's eyes welled with tears and she blinked them away, nodding. Trying to smile. "Of course that means we're back to square one," she said. It was frustrating, but she was more than willing to go back to not knowing if it meant that Claire hadn't suffered at the hands of that sick bastard.

"We aren't quite back to square one," Lucy said slowly, her gaze intent. Giving Emma's hand one last squeeze, she sat back. "We have nothing concrete yet. Not even enough to warrant informing you…"

"But you're going to tell me."

"I need to explain something, first."

"Of course."

Lucy took a sip of her drink, and turned up the corners of her napkin with her free hand.

"Ramsey told you about the case that introduced us—he needed evidence to rule out a female infant abduction as one of Walters's victims and I'd signed out the evidence."

Walters was not Claire's abductor. Still weak with relief, Emma made herself focus on the words Detective Hayes was saying, and nodded.

Claire had not been one of Walters's victims.

She had to call Cal.

"That infant female was my older sister."

Emma's heart lurched as she became fully present. She stared at the detective.

"I don't know exactly what you're going through," Lucy Hayes said. "I never knew my sister. She was abducted before I was born. But I do know how hard it is to live with the aftermath. The way it changes a family. I understand how the not knowing can make you crazy. And give you perpetual hope at the same time."

"Did you find your sister?"

"Not yet. She's the reason I became a cop. So that I could have access to every means possible to find her. My mother…she's never been stable, or even always coherent, since I've known her. She was with Allison at the time she was taken. She was taken, too. The guy beat her up, raped her and left her for dead. But he kept Allison. They never found him. Or my sister."

Holding back the emotion swarming inside her as best she could, Emma asked, "How long was this before you were born?"

"A little over a year."

"So you weren't… The rape didn't make her pregnant."

"No. My father died when I was a baby, though. He was much older than my mother. A cop. She turned to him after Allie was taken. Allie's father, a boyfriend who left her when she found out she was pregnant, was nowhere to be found."

"Was your father on the case?"

"Not full-time. He was from across the state line and followed up on a camera sighting that they thought was my mother and Allie. Turned out not to be, but he checked in on my mom afterward and one thing led to another. He died in an unrelated shoot-out."

"And Allie…your sister…she's not one of Walters's victims either, right? Since you say you haven't found her."

"Right. We don't have Allie's DNA, but a sample from my mother ruled out even a close match."

"My mom's stable," Emma said. "She went back to work a year after Claire went missing. She was a teacher. She's an elementary-school principal now and spends all of her free time advocating for child-safety education. But I've spent my entire life protecting her from the fear and depression that could easily kill her."

The detective nodded, her smile filled with understanding.

"My mother would never have been able to handle my becoming a cop," Emma continued. "Cops were on the list of men I was not to even think about dating because of the possibility someone he put away could get out and come after us."

"Mom didn't like the idea, at first, but when I explained to her that I'd have the best self-defense training around and would be qualified to keep us both safe from harm, she relented. I just don't ever tell her when I'm on a case. She doesn't even know what shifts I work."

"Do you see her often?"

"All the time. She lives across the street from me. She has a part-time caregiver, too. A woman who looks in on her several times a week. Helps her around the house and runs errands for her. I... She drinks and doesn't do well on her own."

Emma felt lucky. "Have you tried to get her into treatment?"

"She's been. Four times. And as soon as something happens that upsets her, she goes right back to the bottle."

"That's got to be rough."

Lucy shrugged. "We manage. She's not a mean drunk. Or a weepy or sloppy one, either. She drinks quietly. At home. And up until recently, she painted. Beautiful landscapes. I've put several of them up on eBay for her and she's actually made pretty good money."

"Why did she stop?"

"She was just in treatment. And she hasn't picked up a brush since she got back."

"Does she live alone?"

"Now she does. There was a guy, Daniel, who lived with us for a long time but he got tired of the drinking, too, and moved out to Arizona. He's got his own construction business out there. He's invited me to visit."

Emma sipped her coffee, not caring that it had gone cold. "Are you going to go?"

"Maybe. I don't take a lot of time off. Except to follow leads off the clock." She grinned. "Too many questions to find answers for, too many cases to be able to leave the job and walk away."

"You should, though," Emma said. "Everyone needs a break now and then."

"That's what Ramsey tells me."

"He takes vacations?"

"No, he just tells me to. Ramsey's one of those guys who knows the rules but doesn't think that they apply to him. Which is part of what makes him a great cop."

"Seems like it could get him into a lot of trouble, not to mention danger."

"He's smart enough to know when to play by the rules even if he doesn't think they apply." Lucy took a long sip of her latte.

Emma was glad the man was on Claire case. Even if, in the end, he brought her b news. It was time to get on with her life.

She'd been in a perpetual holding pat since she was four years old. Waiting to Claire. And somewhere along the wa not knowing had become comfortable though she didn't have her sister wi

she didn't have to mourn. Didn't have to give up hope.

Looking for Claire gave her life meaning. But it was the only real meaning her life held.

And it wasn't enough.

Somehow she had to find a way to let go of the past. One way or another, she needed closure. She had to move on, or she was never going to be happy.

CHAPTER NINETEEN

"I DIDN'T MEAN TO GET so far offtrack." Detective Hayes put her coffee cup down. "You're easy to talk to."

"So are you."

"Thank you." The other woman smiled. "Sometimes I think I get so wrapped up in my work that I forget how to just be a person. You know, I see everyone as a perp or a victim and not as a three-dimensional human being." She chuckled. "Anyway, I have to put my cop hat back on. I wanted to let you know that the possible connection I was working on in Aurora—the one I told you and Cal about—came to nothing."

"Can you tell me what it was?"

"Cal had talked about Claire being a climber. There was a case in Aurora more than twenty years ago, a little girl who'd been abducted from her home. They recovered her, healthy and unharmed, and I remembered reading that when the guy was caught he said that he never would have taken her at all if

the other one hadn't been such a climber.
The detectives on the case discovered that
there'd been another little girl—one the perp
claimed he bought and couldn't remember
from whom. The first child had climbed up
on the kitchen counter, fallen and hit her head
and died. He'd disposed of her body. They'd
recovered some evidence from that first girl,
but hadn't ever been able to make a match
to any missing person's report. Last year she
was added to our DNA database."

"And you know now that it wasn't Claire?"

"That's right."

"Is the guy in prison now?"

"For life. Without parole. And the second
girl he kidnapped is now a senior in college
and doesn't even remember the time away
from her family."

Sometimes justice was done. It was good
to know.

"You said that we weren't quite back to
square one." But it seemed as if they were.

Not that she was complaining. They'd
ruled out two possible homicides this week.
Twice, they'd played Russian roulette and
won.

She was going to have to get something
to eat soon.

To go home to her empty house.

"I believe that Claire might have been in Aurora, Emma."

She froze.

"Not any time recently," the detective clarified, her eyes filled with sympathy.

And suddenly Emma wasn't feeling hungry, or lucky, at all. Was Lucy Hayes about to tell her that Claire was dead, after all?

"About eight years ago there was a big bust in Aurora—a well-to-do woman had been running a black-market adoption operation out of her home on the Ohio River for more than twenty years. She serviced the entire eastern and midwestern United States. And she dealt only with infants up to six months of age."

Emma listened, numbing herself, in case.

"To be honest, I think the bust was part of the reason I moved up to detective so rapidly. I'd been going through my mother's records and found the woman's name and number. Mom told me that some time after detectives failed to turn up any evidence on Allie's whereabouts, she got desperate and went to downtown Cincinnati, to the seamiest part of town, and posed as a desperate young, homeless pregnant woman seeking money in exchange for her unborn baby, hoping to connect with the people who might have sold Allie. Some junkies told her about this woman in Aurora. My mother contacted her, hoping that the woman might remember Allie. The woman told my mother that she'd read about her rape, but that she hadn't had Allie.

"I wasn't quite nineteen at the time, fresh out of the police academy. I told a detective mentor of mine what I knew. I gave her the woman's name and ended up posing as an infertile woman with a lot of cash looking for a newborn, and helped shut the place down."

If Emma hadn't been so preoccupied with wondering how this was going to tie into Claire, she'd have been fascinated. "And you think that Claire was at this woman's house? You think my sister was sold on the black market?"

"I don't think she was sold," the detective said. "But I know that she was at the home at some point."

The din around them faded away. Emma heard pounding in her ears. Waves. And Lucy's voice.

"When the place was busted, they bagged pounds of evidence—baby items, clothes, toys—in the hope that they might be able to trace some of the kids who'd been stolen—or sold by their own parents. I made it my per-

sonal business, with the help of a DNA scientist friend of mine in Cincinnati, to catalog
and file all that evidence."

Emma's heart was pounding so hard she
could barely breathe. She needed fresh air.

"I sent a sample of Claire's DNA to my
friend. I asked her to check it against the
database."

Emma knew. "She found a match."

"Yes." Lucy whispered. She must have.
Emma didn't hear her. But she saw her lips
form the word.

"My sister was adopted. She's alive."

The shake of the detective's head sent her
crashing.

"She's not alive?" Emma asked.

Lucy Hayes frowned. "We don't know. We
might never know. The woman who owned
the mansion kept impeccable records of all
of her adoptions. She kept a little piece of
hair from every baby—they were attached as
identifiers to the records. She gave an iden-
tical record to the adoptive parents, along
with footprints and the forged hospital birth
records. For all intents and purposes, she ran
a legitimate private-adoption agency."

"But none of the hair samples matched
Claire?"

"Uh-huh. We'd already processed all of

the DNA on the hair samples to check them against cold-case missing-child cases. There was no evidence of Allie there, either, but I was able to solve a couple of other cases from what we found."

"I can see why you don't take vacations."

"I know, I'm obsessed. I admit it. I'm addicted to finding children just like my mother is addicted to alcohol. I come by the addictive personality naturally. But at least I'm using it constructively."

"Hey, I'm not criticizing!" Emma said. "You've done so much more than I ever have. I admire you." Lucy Hayes had a life.

"Yeah, well, don't forget, Emma, I didn't know my sister. You knew and loved yours. More than that, you were the big sister, and to a four-year-old, that means Claire was your baby."

Lucy was right. She had felt like Claire was her baby as well as Rose's. But no one else had ever said so. Herself included.

"So what do you think it means? Claire having been there? I mean, if she wasn't adopted out, why would she have been there at all?"

"I'm not sure. The agency handled only newborns and Claire would have been at least two. Maybe the woman tried to find a buyer for her and couldn't."

"What would have happened to her, then?"

Lucy Hayes gave her a look that made Emma go cold. "You think they might have killed her?"

"I'm not going there. Not unless I have to. At this point, there's been no evidence of any murders. To the contrary, the babies in the woman's care were well cared for. The mansion has been torn down, the land redeveloped. If there were bodies there, they'd have been found already."

"So what happens next?"

"I keep looking," Lucy said. "I go through all of the evidence of that case again, comparing what's there with what I know about Claire. I talk to anyone else I can find who might know more about what went on in that house. I question the adoptive parents again. I'll go over all of the trial transcripts, too. Once I'm fully versed in the case, I'll head to prison to talk to the woman again."

"That sounds like more work than one person can accomplish."

"It's not as onerous as it sounds. I have it down to a system. And Ramsey will be helping me."

"I don't know how I'll ever repay you."

"You won't. I'm just doing my job, Emma. Because this has to do with the Aurora bust, my department will pay me. Not many people get paid to feed their addictions, you know?" The detective smiled, but her eyes told another story.

"I could have waited to fill you in until I knew more, but I had a feeling you'd want to be kept informed every step of the way."

"You're right," Emma said, pulling her purse back up to her shoulder as Detective Hayes stood. "Thank you."

"No need to thank me, either." Lucy Hayes handed her a card. "Call me if you think of anything else that might help me narrow my search."

"I will." Emma walked with the woman to the door.

"And call me if you just want to talk, too," the detective added, turning to look at Emma. "I mean that."

Emma nodded. "That goes both ways," she said, thinking that as difficult as facing up to life was, it wasn't all bad. For the first time in twenty-five years she'd met someone who knew what she had gone through. Someone who knew what it was like to walk around with an open wound in your core. Someone who not only understood her intellectually, but who could relate to her emotionally, too.

For the first time since she'd lost Claire, she no longer felt completely and utterly alone.

CHAPTER TWENTY

EMMA MEANT TO GO straight home after her meeting with the detective. She'd like to have gone to her mother's, to share what she'd learned about Claire, but she'd never been able to trust Rose when it came to her little sister. Her mother would insist on visiting the woman from Aurora in prison. She'd stop at nothing to find out why Claire had been in that home.

She'd want to do everything Lucy Hayes was doing for them, and she'd likely go without sleeping or eating in the process.

"You've reached Cal Whittier. Please leave a message."

Sitting in her parked car outside of the Caffeine Café, Emma said, "Hey, big brother, it's me. I just met with Detective Hayes. Walters didn't have Claire, Cal...." She paused as tears choked her up, and then, swallowing, said, "They did get a hit on the DNA, though. They don't have anything solid, but they believe that at some point Claire was in a house in Aurora where black-market adoptions were conducted, but they don't think Claire was adopted. Anyway, call me when you get a chance."

She hung up and stared out at the bustling street, the couples holding hands, harried women with seemingly important places to be.

She brought up a virtual notepad on her cell phone. She had a journal entry to make. One that she'd copy into her book when she got home.

3. I need other women in my life—and their presence won't make me disloyal to my mother or to Claire.

Closing the notepad function, she knew that she'd found another self-truth.

Now she had to figure out what to do with the rest of this Friday night.

There were plenty of things she could do. Places she could go. Even teacher friends she could call who would be happy to see a movie with her or catch up over dinner. She could do some quilting, or lesson planning. She had project booklets to create for the senior-class trip to Washington, D.C., in December.

What she wanted to do was drink a glass of wine and listen to piano music.

She had to call Chris before he just stopped by her house again. With another home pregnancy test.

And if he did, would she send him away?

Emma didn't trust herself to do so. She also didn't want him to have her number. She didn't want to be able to hope that he'd call her.

She had to see him. On neutral ground. With other people around. So she'd keep her clothes on.

She had to make sure he didn't show up at her door again.

But what about the wine? What if Chris was right and she was pregnant? She couldn't drink if she was pregnant.

Oh, God. She couldn't be pregnant. She just couldn't handle any more right now. Her period wasn't even late.

Still, just in case, she'd stick with tea.

CHRIS SIPPED HIS beer slowly, watching Cody make drinks, clean glasses and carry on conversations that made his customers feel important all at the same time. Don Carmine had one hell of an employee in that young man.

"I thought you'd be playing tonight." The

statement came from behind Chris and he swung around, not liking the way that voice made him feel, as though he'd just brought in a week's worth of lobster in a day. "Emma."

She shouldn't be there. Not with him there. It was why he'd called. They shouldn't be seen together.

"Did you get my message?"

"Yeah." She looked far too good in her proper teacher clothes. And the way her hair was tied back only made him itch to untie it, to see those dark curls fan out around her.

He had it bad.

And she had to stay away from him for another reason. He'd had a visitor at the dock earlier that evening. He'd been threatened. And he didn't think the threat was an idle one.

Chris wasn't afraid for himself. He was afraid for Emma. But he didn't believe anything would happen to her in public.

"Have a seat." He pulled out the stool next to him. She was there now. If she'd been seen with him, it was already too late. And he had to let her know why he'd called. He had to let her know what was going on.

Cody appeared with a glass of white wine, but Emma shook her head. "I'll just have tea," she said.

Chris's muscles tensed up. Leaning over so that only she would hear, he asked, "Are you starting to feel pregnant?"

The quick shake of her head wasn't very reassuring.

"You worried yet?"

"No." She looked him straight in the eye. "There's nothing to worry about, Chris," she said, and he began to wonder if she was trying to convince him, or herself. "I have your phone number now so I can call you and let you know when you're off the hook."

"It's not just me on the hook," he reminded her.

"I know. I didn't mean… I just… I'm not your concern and there's no reason why I should be and—"

He didn't like her brush-off any better than he liked the fact that she had showed up tonight.

"What do you mean, you aren't my concern? I'm very concerned about the effect any repercussions from our night together would have on you."

Her silence shut him out. He didn't want her to shut him out.

"Are you playing in the competition tonight?" she asked, motioning toward the dais. "Have you been up already?"

"No. I was late tonight. Missed getting a number."

"You're just here to drink?"

I'm here because I'd hoped you'd show up.
"I'll play as soon as the competition wraps up. It's kind of a standing arrangement."

She grinned. "You get the piano anytime you want, you mean."

Shrugging, Chris took another sip of beer. She felt good. Being with her felt good.

Just for the moment.

The door opened and a tall, thin man entered. He had short dark hair and was wearing a business suit.

Chris's first instinct was to grab Emma's hand and head out the back way.

"What?" she asked, and glancing back at her he saw her looking between him and the stranger who'd just walked in.

"I thought I recognized him, but I was wrong."

"I think I feel sorry for whoever you thought he was," Emma told him, her brow furrowed.

Chris sipped his beer, sized her up and said, "That's actually what I called you about."

"I thought you called to find out what my doctor said."

"Someone was waiting for me at the dock this evening."

"Excuse me?"

"Rob Evert came to see me."

Emma stiffened, her expression changing her into a woman he hardly recognized. "Rob came to see you? Whatever for?"

"He says you're engaged to him."

"He's lying." The words were unequivocal.

"I had a feeling he was," Chris told her. "But I'm guessing it's his ring that left that white mark on your finger."

She took her left hand off the bar and slid it under her thigh. "Yeah. He's the guy I told you about."

"The one you found fooling around that first day we met?"

"Right."

Chris hadn't liked the guy even before he'd known who he was. Hadn't liked the ego that preceded him by about two feet. Once the guy had introduced himself, his dislike had turned to disgust.

"He warned me to stay away from you, Emma."

"He had no business doing that."

"I figured as much. But he wasn't in any frame of mind to be reasonable."

"What did he do?"

"It's not so much what he did as how he did it. He was clearly agitated and he let me know, in no uncertain terms, that if I didn't stay away from you, he'd make certain that you stayed away from me."

Frowning, Emma asked, "How did he even know to find you?"

"At first I thought you told him where I worked. But he said something about watching you and your house. Like he's appointed himself your bodyguard."

Emma's mouth dropped open. "You're kidding."

"I wish I was. There was something not quite right about him. Like he wasn't quite stable. And it sounds as if he's been following you, or having you followed, since you broke it off. He knew about both the times I'd been at your house."

"I can't believe this. Rob was possessive, but not like this. It doesn't even make sense to me. He's never shown any signs of being... unstable."

"Maybe because you've never broken up with him before. I'm telling you, to hear the guy talk, you all have set a date and are sending out invitations. If things are as you said, if you've told him you want nothing more to do with him, then I think you should call the police."

"ON ROB?" EMMA could hardly believe what she was hearing. "I figured he wouldn't give up easily," she said. "Rob has a hard time letting go of what he believes is his. But I've never been afraid of him."

It was an odd thought that her ex-fiancé was watching her. She would never have guessed he'd waste his time that way.

"I should have called the cops immediately," Chris said, "but I didn't think you were in any immediate danger, as long as I kept away from you, and I wanted to speak with you first. I called you as soon as he left and I've been waiting for your return call. But now you're here. He probably knows that we're together, and I won't feel right about you walking out of here. I really think we should file a report."

She thought of calling Lucy Hayes. She was comfortable with the detective. Trusted her not to overreact. But they were way out of the female detective's jurisdiction.

Besides, Lucy was heading back to Aurora that weekend.

"I'm telling you, this wasn't just a fit of

jealousy," Chris said. Emma loved his voice. And the concerned look in his eyes as he watched her. She didn't want to be afraid.

She was tired of being afraid.

"He just doesn't know how to take rejection." Emma tried to explain the man she'd spent many years with—the man she'd planned to marry. Rob had his faults, but he'd had some really good qualities, too. "He's not used to losing at anything." Neither was he a violent man.

Or a vindictive one.

"I got the sense that this was about more than jealousy or ego," Chris continued, "although he had more than his share of the latter. He said he'd put in five years and had too much at stake to let you walk away from him. He said he isn't going to let someone else collect what he's earned. It didn't sound as if he was referring to your heart."

"That makes no sense to me. I'm a teacher. My mother is a principal, and her salary was recently cut. We do fine, but any extra money we have is spent on our efforts campaigning. We have no savings at all. Rob knows all of that."

"I'm just telling you what I heard," Chris was saying. His serious expression, the tone of his voice, was scaring her. "I can't make you go to the police, but if you don't, I'm going to call and make a report."

"Okay, I'll contact them," Emma said. At least that way she'd have some control. "I'd like to give Detective Ramsey Miller a call, if you don't mind. He's with the Comfort Cove Police Department."

"Is he working on your sister's case?"

"Yeah. So maybe this is out of his jurisdiction, but he'll know who we should talk to."

"Fine." Chris's chin jutted as he gave a short nod. "Can you call him now?"

"Tonight?"

"This guy could be outside right now. Or at your house. Waiting. I'd feel better if the cops knew where he was. Especially now that we've disregarded his warning."

Emma pulled her phone out of her purse. Calling the police on Rob? She couldn't believe she was doing this.

And wondered if there was something the matter with her that she couldn't seem to say no to this fisherman.

CHAPTER TWENTY-ONE

DETECTIVE RAMSEY MILLER was okay with following leads that led to dead ends. Leads that forced him to considerate alternate paths. He was okay with questions that came without obvious answers. With working every hour of every day that God gave him.

He wasn't okay with little girls disappearing without a trace.

"What we have here is missing forensic evidence and forensic evidence turning up in a black-market baby ring in Aurora." Lucy Hayes looked at him from across the conference table in the squad room after-hours on Friday night and summed up the day's progress. Folders and transcripts and scraps of paper covered the scarred old table.

She was due to fly out of Boston on Sunday. They had a lot to do between now and then.

Claire Sanderson was not one of Walters's victims. For that he was thankful.

"Let's say whoever took the evidence also

planted it at Mrs. Buckley's place," Ramsey supposed out loud. The seventy-year-old woman who'd been locked up for eight years had sworn to them by conference call that evening that she knew nothing about a toddler girl in her home twenty-five years before.

"I dealt only with newborns," she'd insisted, confessing only that much off the record, even after they'd hinted at a deal—giving her a chance at a lesser sentence, and maybe some immunity—if she was able to help them solve this crime.

"You think whoever took the box of Claire's evidence from your vault also knew about Buckley's operation?" Lucy grabbed their copies of the baby photos that had been confiscated from the Buckley mansion, studying them again.

Ramsey had had their sketch artist play around with the photos they had of Claire Sanderson to see if he could find any evidence of a likeness to Claire among the Buckley photos.

"Maybe the thief wants us to think that Claire was adopted."

"Maybe she *was* adopted," Lucy said, staring at Ramsey. "Maybe what we have here is a baby who was stolen, adopted by Rose

Sanderson, and then taken back. For whatever reason."

"Like maybe a biological father who didn't know he had a daughter until too late and then wanted her back." He ran with the theory.

"Or a mother who was young, or even not so young, whose circumstances changed, who regretted giving up her baby, knew she had no legal recourse since she'd sold her child illegally, but felt she had a right to raise her own child." Lucy watched him.

"And if Rose Sanderson knew she bought the baby illegally, she wasn't likely to put the police on Buckley's trail." They could have something here. "Do you know if anyone actually saw Rose pregnant with Claire?"

"It's not on record but I doubt the question was ever asked."

Lucy's expression changed from wide-eyed anticipation to disappointment. "But if she wasn't putting the police on Buckley's trail for fear of being found out, why would she put the police on any trail at all?"

"Because she fell in love with the baby she adopted? Because she sees Claire as her own?"

The woman across from him riffled through the piles of paperwork on the table and came up with a legal-looking document. "A copy of Claire Sanderson's birth certificate."

Ramsey produced a folder. "Copies of all of the forged birth certificates."

Lucy smiled. "Claire's could be fake."

"And this whole theory could easily be disproven," Ramsey realized.

"With the DNA sample from Emma Sanderson," Lucy finished for him. Too bad the detective lived a few states away. She thought enough like him to be a damned good partner.

Shawn had called with the results of the test, telling them only that Claire hadn't been a match for Walters, but he'd offered to fax a full report over that evening. Ramsey went to see if it had come in. Lucy was studying the Buckley report when he returned.

"That theory's dead," he said. "Claire Sanderson's DNA was a close match to Emma's. Shawn says there's no doubt that the two are closely related."

"Okay, well, Mrs. Buckley had clients as far south as Florida and as far north as Maine," Lucy said. "She also had several from Massachusetts, which means that the people involved in this kind of thing in Massachusetts knew about her, right? Maybe the guy who took Claire didn't realize that Buckley only dealt with newborns. Maybe he took Claire to Buckley, but, ultimately, didn't sell her there."

"Or maybe he knew, but hoped to persuade her otherwise and failed."

"Buckley was pretty adamant that she'd never seen Claire."

"She could be lying, but why?"

He shook his head.

"Could be that Claire's abductor found out about Buckley's arrest, knew about the DNA samples that police were able to get from the woman's house and was afraid those samples would lead police to Claire Sanderson."

Ramsey dissected the theory on the spot. "That would be motive for stealing the box of evidence from our vault," he said. "Buckley's been in jail for years, but we have no idea how long the box of evidence has been missing."

"Do you have a record of everyone going in and out of the storage room here? As you've said all along, chances are good that whoever took that evidence had an inside connection."

Ramsey dug through his piles and came up with the folder.

Lucy took it from him. "I'll go through

the report from the Buckley case and we can compare the two. Maybe we'll get lucky."

She smiled as though her team had just scored a home run.

Ramsey studied her. "All of this work, the years of searching—and other than the original police report on your sister, you've found nothing. Don't you ever want to give up?"

Lucy looked him in the eye. "Would you?"

"I wouldn't know," he said. "I've never had a sibling, or a child, to know what losing one feels like."

"You lost your wife, Miller, when she left you. That counts."

He'd seen Hayes's determination to get to the truth. And he wasn't going to find himself on the other end of that. "Then, no, I wouldn't quit until I had my answers."

His phone rang. He was glad for the diversion.

"Miller."

He glanced at Lucy as he recognized the name of his caller. And when he heard the reason for the call, he knew it was going to be another long night.

"I DON'T LIKE this." Lucy Hayes, dressed in plain clothes in Emma's living room Saturday afternoon, directed her comment to Detective Miller.

Chris was siding with her. He didn't like Miller's plan at all.

"Are you objecting on the grounds that the plan doesn't have merit or because you're feeling protective?" Miller said to the other detective.

Lucy raised her chin. "I'm objecting because I don't like it," she said. "We have an overjealous ex, who must be watched, I agree. But to use Emma to get him to incriminate himself? I don't like it."

Chris had received Emma's message regarding this meeting when he'd returned to shore that afternoon. He'd come straight from the docks, without taking the time to change the shorts and T-shirt he'd worn under his coveralls all day.

"You saw how he was last night," Miller said, leaning away from Chris and Emma. "We each took our shot at him and came up empty."

After he'd received Emma's call the night before, Miller had picked up Rob Evert for questioning on a possible harassment charge.

Miller faced Emma and Chris, who were sitting on opposite ends of the couch. "Last night wasn't the first time Evert was uncooperative. We approached him after we met with Emma and Cal on Monday. Because he was close with the family, we wanted to talk to him. To see if he could shed any new light or perspective on the work Emma and her mother do, or provide us with any leads as to who could have taken that box of evidence. He refused to speak with us."

"Rob wouldn't talk to you after Cal and I met with you?" Even now Emma seemed surprised by the man's actions. Which made her that much more vulnerable as far as Chris was concerned.

"He said not to bother him again unless we had a warrant or subpoena," Detective Hayes said softly. "I assumed he reacted that way because you'd recently broken up with him, but now I'm not so sure. Why would he think we'd want to get a warrant or subpoena?"

"And considering Chris's account of his interaction with Evert, combined with Evert's uncooperative behavior when we picked him up for questioning last night, I believe we should use all available means to find out what this guy's up to," Miller said.

"Rob didn't have anything to do with Claire's disappearance, that's for sure," Emma said, pulling her hair back into a ponytail and wrapping it with an elastic band from around her wrist. "He was only six at the time."

"We already had him checked out," Hayes said. "We had someone on that on Tuesday and nothing turned up."

"Rob grew up in Idaho," Emma said. "He moved to Boston on a basketball scholarship and ended up settling here in Comfort Cove."

The female detective nodded. "And every bit of that checks out."

"There's something the guy doesn't want us to know," Miller said to the room at large. "Am I the only one here who wants to find out what that is?"

"No." Emma rubbed her hands along her jeans. "I'll do whatever it takes to figure out what's going on. I'm shocked that he refused to speak with you earlier in the week. He's always been completely supportive of our efforts to find Claire."

"I believe he's hiding something, as well," Hayes said. "I just don't like involving Emma in this."

"I'm the only one he's interested in. Who else could do this but me?" Emma focused on the female detective. "Like you posing as a wealthy infertile woman for the Buckley case."

Emma wasn't backing down. Chris admired her bravery—and didn't like it one bit.

She'd gone from the best one-night stand of his life to a regular fixture.

And the more he tried to get her out of his life, the more deeply entangled they became.

Sara would make a mountain out of this one. Which was why he was never, ever going to be stupid enough to tell her about Emma.

"We can keep a watch on him, wait for something to turn up, hope that he makes a mistake, turns his hand—"

"—but that could take months. Or never happen," Emma broke in, her beautiful face lined with a mixture of concern, frustration, fear. "I don't think Rob would hurt me, or anyone, really, but after what he said to Chris, I just don't know anymore. I'd rather find out what's going on than to have to spend days and weeks worrying about what he might be up to. Or to have him stalking me. I can't leave town, or afford a bodyguard. And if there's any chance that what he's doing has any connection to Claire, then..."

Chris wasn't going to win this one.

"I'm in," he said.

"I WANT TO get this over with as quickly as possible," Emma said. Sharing her couch with Chris Talbot was getting to be a habit, she thought. And that had to end as quickly as possible, too. "It seems to me that having Chris openly around is the way to do it. I can approach Rob myself, try to draw him out, but he's not going to open up to me. I lived with the man for two years and I can't imagine what he thinks I have that would be worth anything to him."

"You're worth far more than anything he could ever have."

Emma stared at Chris. Had he really just said what she'd thought he'd said? If so, he gave no indication of that fact. "Like I told you last night, I'm pretty certain that the guy was feeling threatened by a possible loss of something substantial," Chris said to the detectives. "I wish I could remember his exact words, but it was something about having put in almost five years of his life and not letting someone else waltz in and get what he'd earned."

What a fool she'd been. What a fool fear had made her. "He was always so supportive…" she said aloud. She'd made a mess of things. She looked to Lucy. "I'm a bit of a worrywart," she said, and was grateful when the female detective's gaze softened, though she'd have continued either way. "Rob was very patient with me. He never criticized me for being so careful. And he was just as supportive of my mother. He never complained about her clinginess. It's hard for me to believe that was all an act."

"Could be that's what he meant by putting in his time," Ramsey Miller said.

Lucy frowned. "But what would he 'earn'? What could he possibly think he'd lost?"

"Are you due to inherit any money? Or come into some kind of settlement? Something to do with Claire, maybe?"

"No." Emma would have laughed if the situation wasn't so tragic. Laughed without humor. "Mom had to file bankruptcy a few years ago because of all the debt she'd accrued. Rob knew about it. There's no money in our family."

Lucy sat forward in her chair. "What about your grandfather in Florida?"

"He lives on social security."

"So maybe Evert knows something you don't know," Miller said. "Or thinks he does."

"I can't imagine what it would be. Our whole lives, other than work, revolve around Claire. This has something to do with her. There's simply nothing else."

"I was on my way back to Indiana tomorrow, but I can ask for a couple of extra days and stay here with Emma," Lucy said.

"Too obvious." Miller shook his head, looking at Lucy. "Evert saw you last night."

"I'll stay." Chris's words came from beside her.

Emma heard him clear down to her toes.

"We want the guy to believe I ignored his warning. To think that Emma and I are getting hot and heavy…"

"Which, for the record, we're not," Emma stated emphatically to the detectives. She didn't want them to get the wrong idea.

"Which we're not," Chris agreed, and then said, "but if we want him to think we are, then it makes sense that I stay here for a few days. Or nights, rather. I have to work during the day."

"Right." Emma glanced over at him and then back to Lucy and Miller. "He's self-employed. He has to work."

Miller nodded and pinned Emma with a stare that would have scared her if she didn't know he was on her side. "I'm going to have specific rules for you to follow," he said. "If I hear that you are not following them to the letter, I will call an end to the operation."

She nodded. "You have nothing to worry about on that score, Detective," she said with a self-deprecating chuckle. "Rules are the one thing I've lived successfully with my entire life."

After Emma and Chris agreed to the plan the department had already approved, the detectives assured them that plain-clothes officers would be watching Emma, and regular duty officers would do random drive-bys past her house. For the next few days she wasn't to leave her house without checking in. And she wasn't to be without a recording device at any time. They would be putting a tap on her phone.

"My captain has given us the go-ahead from the cold case budget," Miller said. "With the missing evidence box, Evert's uncharacteristic threats, his insistence that he's earned something from you, his stalking—we need to know what he's up to. And since he's unwilling to cooperate…"

"And—" Lucy Hayes reached over for Emma's hand "—you have to be prepared here, Emma. We could be dealing with murder and we just don't know it yet. Someone could be covering up your sister's murder."

"That's right," Miller jumped in. "Rob clearly wants something. And whoever stole that evidence is trying very hard to keep us from finding something. Something they might be willing to spend a lot of money to keep quiet. Maybe they're paying Rob. Maybe not. Kidnapping is a serious charge. Murder even more so. Could be that the kidnapper is afraid of being discovered and will do whatever it takes to stay out of jail. We're only supposing here, but Detective Hayes and I have a lot of collective experience between us and this looks serious."

CHAPTER TWENTY-TWO

THE PLAN WAS FOR CHRIS and Emma to spend that night together, to meet up again after Chris finished work on Sunday and then regroup with Ramsey on Monday. Hayes was heading back to Indiana tomorrow as planned.

In the meantime police personnel were running a full check on Evert's phone records and contacts, and canvassing the accounting firm where he worked, as well as his known hangouts, for anything that might shed light on their investigation.

The whole thing left Chris uneasy. He didn't like the idea of exposing Emma to whatever Evert might have in store. The guy knew her well, knew her vulnerabilities. And felt no shame in using them to manipulate her. Chris also didn't put it past the guy to harm her physically, if doing so would serve his end.

Clearly Chris had seen a different side to the man. A side Emma had never seen.

Emma locked the door behind the detectives.

He had to ask.

"Did you get your period?"

"No."

She explained that she wanted to see her own doctor. And while the wait wasn't easy, he understood.

Chris needed a shower.

They could shower together. He pictured her firm breasts with beads of water on them. And got hard.

Like some horny teenager.

"I invited my mother for dinner tonight." She stood in the foyer, looking as uncomfortable as he felt.

"And you don't want her to meet me."

Her eyes shadowed, but she said, "It wouldn't be a good idea."

He understood. "I'll leave. Come back later tonight."

Emma wrapped her arms around the breasts he'd just been fantasizing about. "I don't think that would be a good idea. If Rob's watching he'd know two things. First, that you aren't spending time with Mom when I am, and that would tell him that I'm not serious about you. And second, that Mom and I are here, alone, and he might see that as his opportunity to try to get back in with us. I don't want Mom involved in this at all. I'll call her and cancel."

"You aren't going to tell her what we're up to?"

"Absolutely not."

"Don't you think you should? What if she stops by?"

"She doesn't ever stop here without calling first. It's her way of giving me space. And, believe me, it's best not to tell her. She'd be worried sick and there's nothing she can do. Which wouldn't stop her from coming up with her own plan and acting on it."

"Maybe it would help you to share some of the stress with her."

"No," she said adamantly. "All I'd be doing is opening myself to weeks, possibly months, of her paranoia where I'm concerned. Constantly checking on me to see that I'm okay. Repeatedly warning me about every dire possibility."

"Is it really that extreme?"

"It really is."

Chris had the impression that things were even worse than Emma was portraying them.

He wanted to make them better.

Which was ludicrous.

As was handling her with kid gloves. Emma was a strong, capable woman.

So they were going to spend this time together. And then they'd part ways. He couldn't go on pretending to be something he was not.

"I need a shower."

"There are fresh towels in my bathroom. Or you can use the spare bathroom upstairs."

"I was thinking more along the lines of using my own. We could drive to my place and then have dinner out before heading back here for the night."

He knew he was making a mistake even as he said the words. That didn't stifle them. He didn't take people to his house. Ever. A sick feeling came over him as she agreed to the plan.

Which was partially why he said what he said next.

"And tomorrow, I think you should come out on the boat with me." He didn't like leaving her alone—even with police protection. And he had to get her into his world, to see and understand her distaste for it so they could get past whatever this thing was between them. "I don't like the idea of you here all by yourself until we find out exactly what Evert's doing."

"What if I get seasick?"

"Then you hang your head overboard. The fish won't care. I have plenty of towels. And believe me, nothing is noticeable over the smell of the catch."

"You ever been sick out there before?"

It took him a second to realize she wasn't saying no. She wasn't backing away.

He smiled. "Hell, yeah, I've been sick. More than once. And not just as a kid, although I had my share of miserable moments back when I first started going out with my dad."

"So you speak from experience."

"Yep."

"I'm not sure I have the proper attire, but I'm game," she said before he could rethink the wisdom of taking her out on the water with him.

"I'll rustle up some small coveralls," he said, remembering Sara. Her whole future had rested on her liking it out on the water. She'd wanted to like it more than anything.

She'd had nothing against the docks. And she'd loved the ocean.

She'd hated lobstering. Hated it enough to leave him over it. She didn't want to stay onshore alone and she didn't want to go out with him, either.

And he couldn't give it up.

Emma said something about collecting her purse and keys. They were going to ride together in his truck.

He eyed her backside as she left the room.

And, remembering Sara's reaction to the haul, he figured he was going to be just fine.

Of course they'd had sex again that night, too. It didn't mean anything. They'd used a condom. There was always the possibility that having sex would make her start her period. And as soon as Rob's intentions were revealed, which she hoped would be soon, and Emma started her period, which would also be soon, they would say their goodbyes and Chris Talbot would be nothing more than a sweet memory.

A man she'd remember every time she heard piano music.

Feeling bulky and unattractive in the gold-colored, stained coveralls he'd borrowed for her, she stood on the dock before dawn Sunday morning watching as he readied his bait—herring that he'd brought down from Manny's in a large plastic tray—and made a quick check of the *Son Catcher* before they headed out. She was putting off for as long as possible the moment when she'd have to climb aboard.

And thinking about last night only so that she didn't panic and chicken out.

Going to bed with Chris just got better and better. The night before, she'd fallen asleep in his arms knowing full well that she'd be waking in them, as well. The fact that she'd had a nightmare-free slumber might or might not have had anything to do with him.

But it didn't matter either way.

Chris was a fisherman. Even with her new outlook, her determination to change the way she lived, she knew better than to think she could take on a life that encompassed real danger every day.

Danger aside, Chris was forty years old. And he didn't want a family.

"You ready?" He squinted up at her, the dock light putting his face in stark relief.

Her heart tripped. Because of what she was about to do? Or because of who she was about to do it with?

"Crazy that getting on this boat with you seems more wrong than going back to your hotel room to get naked." She was nervous. Babbling.

"Give me your hand." She took the palm

he offered. And when she felt his slight tug, she stepped down into the boat.

FIVE MINUTES INTO the ride Emma would have given everything she owned to be back at Chris's house instead.

She'd never have pictured him to live in a place like that quaint, glorious cottage on the cliff, where he'd taken her the night before. Not that she'd seen much of it. He'd sat her in the kitchen, at the bay window overlooking the ocean, and picked her up there less than ten minutes later, walking her right back out the door they'd come through.

She'd loved the view from up on the cliff. Out on the ocean, she still loved the view. But she was going to throw up.

CHAPTER TWENTY-THREE

"HOLD ON TO THE SIDE rail." Chris gripped the trap's rope with one hand and Emma's wrist with the other, knowing that if he let go of either one, someone could die.

He'd already pulled up the buoy and had the trap halfway up when Emma had hurled herself to the side of the boat again, retching so violently she lost her balance. He'd turned to catch her before she pitched overboard and got his left ankle caught in the trap's rope. If he let go, he was going back down with the trap.

"Easy," he said, his right arm burning with the effort it was taking to hold on to his trap. "You're okay. I've got you."

She'd already thrown up twice. For her sake he hoped this was the last time. Her ribs had to be bruised, though she'd yet to complain. "It'll just be dry heaves soon," he said. "You can't have that much more in your stomach."

They'd had toast and coffee for breakfast. Dry toast, in case of this eventuality. It hadn't helped. Nor had the ear patch he'd given her—a sometime remedy for seasickness. He should have insisted she take the antinausea pill, but he'd been unsure what effect it would have on a fetus if she was pregnant.

"Uh." Emma hung her upper body over the side of the vessel as though she didn't have enough energy to right herself.

"Deep breaths," he told her. "It'll be better soon."

He hoped. Unless she was pregnant and what they were seeing was a horrible combination of sea and morning sicknesses.

"I'm so sorry," she said, and glanced sideways. "Oh, no, you're in the middle of hauling up a trap!" Emma stood and reached for the rope. "I didn't realize you'd pulled up the buoy! The rope's around your ankle."

Before he could react she'd freed herself from his grasp and was down on the deck of the boat, helping to untangle him from the rope that could have taken him overboard.

The catch was good—worth a burning arm—and Chris worked swiftly, measuring the carapace of the lobsters with his steel gauge, throwing back the ones that were too small or too large, and then rebaiting the trap before sending it back down.

He turned, ready to band the claws, and found Emma a step ahead of him, using the banding tool to apply the elastic rubber band to the lobster in her gloved grasp. It wasn't easy work. Or for the queasy or fearful. It took her a bit longer than it would have taken him, but she'd mastered the skill faster than he had his first time out.

"I can do that," he said. "You should rest...."

"I can do it, too, Chris. I need to stay busy— if I just sit here I feel worse. And besides, you need to be steering this thing to the next stop. You're not going to have time to get all your work done before the sun goes down."

"You amaze me," he told Emma, watching her for a second.

She wrinkled her forehead. "Why? Because I can learn a new skill?" She grunted as she wrestled with another lobster.

"No. Because you puke and pop right back up," he said. "You spend twenty-five years looking for your sister and still have the ability to believe that she might be alive. Do you ever give up?"

"Oh, no, you don't, buddy." Emma repositioned the lobster, which had almost slipped from the clasp she had around his claws.

"I give up," she answered him in the next breath. "Ask Rob. I gave up on him."

Dropping the banded lobster in the bin, Emma moved on to the next one.

And Chris moved on, too. She was right; he was behind schedule.

THERE WAS A missed call from Rob on Emma's cell phone when she returned to shore late Sunday afternoon. There was one from Cal, too. She had aches and pains in every place her body had sensation. Her arms and shoulders throbbed, her ribs cried out every time she moved. And even though she'd been wearing gloves, the lobster pinches had still managed to bruise a couple of her fingers.

"I stink," she announced, dropping her phone back into her purse. Shower first, then voice mail. Right after Chris sold his catch and took care of the rest of his business at the dock.

"You want to head straight back to your place as soon as I'm done here?"

She wanted to head straight to bed with him. "Yes, please. I thought I'd make a big Caesar salad with French bread for dinner tonight. How does that sound?"

As soon as the question left her mouth, she realized how much it sounded as if they were an old married couple and she promptly lost her appetite. Hopefully her call from Rob would garner Ramsey whatever information he needed so that she and Chris could end this charade.

"How about fresh lobster salad?" he called from the deck of the boat.

Right. They'd just come back with a full cargo of lobster. "I don't know how to prepare lobster."

"Then I guess we'll have to make dinner together."

Emma started to shake—and she wasn't the least bit cold. She was petrified. The man wanted to cook with her.

Which was her idea of a perfect date.

"HEY, MILLER, I'VE got your results."

Another possible victim of Walters's.

Looking up from his desk, Ramsey studied the face of the forensic scientist coming toward him. Shawn was a good kid. A hard worker. Based in the Boston lab, Shawn didn't complain about the extra hours Ramsey caused for him in Comfort Cove. Ramsey's biggest problem with the guy was his fear that Shawn hero-worshipped him.

For a scientist, the kid sure was slow to discover that Ramsey's feet were made of clay.

Right now, Shawn didn't appear to have discovered anything. His face was a blank slate.

The back of Ramsey's neck tensed.

With one last glance at the skinny, bespectacled young man, he reached for the folder Shawn held out, opened it and read.

There'd been another positive identification of victims' belongings found in Peter Walters's basement.

At four o'clock on Sunday, Ramsey Miller tucked a stack of folders under his arm and left the office.

"EMMA, BABE, PLEASE call me back. It's important." Waiting in Chris's truck while he conducted his business with Manny, Emma punched the button to save Rob's voice-mail message and listened for the second new message to play.

"Hi, Em, it's Cal. Great news about Claire. Great news. Please call when you can. Morgan wants to meet you. We were thinking about taking a trip up to Comfort Cove during fall break. Call me."

She listened to Cal's message a second time with tears in her eyes. It was so hard to believe that she had her big brother back after twenty-five years. Someone who'd known her before Claire was taken, someone who was there that horrible day that changed their lives for eternity.

"ROB CALLED," EMMA said as Chris climbed into his truck, holding their wrapped dinner in his hand.

His gaze shot to her face, trying to get a read on her emotional state. "What did he say?"

"Nothing. He just asked me to call, said it was important."

"He didn't sound agitated, or upset?"

"Nope." Emma's ponytail swung from side to side as she shook her head. "He sounded completely normal. It was pretty much like every other call I've had from him in the past three weeks."

That glorious hair was his downfall. If she'd just cut it off he'd be fine.

"Did you call him back yet?"

"No, and I don't intend to."

"Good. Miller said if Rob contacted you to call him before you did anything."

"Detective Miller also said to act normal, to do what I'd normally do, so as not to tip off Rob."

"So what *would* you normally do?"

She shrugged. "He's been calling for three weeks now. And for three weeks I've been ignoring him. It's going to frustrate him more if I continue to ignore him. We need him to think he's lost all hold on me."

She was right. And he should have reached the same conclusion.

"But you're still checking in with Miller, right?"

Pushing the speed-dial button on her phone, Emma did as Chris asked. Miller agreed with her that the best defense was to ignore Rob's call.

And so they were off to her place.

Chris had packed a change of clothes the night before, and almost wished he hadn't. Wished he had an excuse to go back to his own house, even if he couldn't stay.

ALMOST AS IF they'd had some tacit agreement, Emma faced her room at the top of the stairs and Chris pointed in the direction of the spare bathroom. "You said you have towels in there?" he asked, his overnight bag in his hand.

"Yes."

"I'll meet you downstairs, then."

They weren't showering together. They

couldn't. It was entirely too intimate—more intimate than sex, even.

But the idea of running a washcloth all over Chris's body, of having him standing before her so that she could see every part of him at once, had Emma reaching for the cold-water tap.

She made sure to check that she had clean sheets on her spare bed, too.

Chris was already in the kitchen, a pot of water on the stove, the two-pound lobster in the sink behind him, when Emma came downstairs.

"Do you have to cut its head off or remove the shell before you cook it?" she asked, staring into the open eyes of the critter.

"Nope. I've already scrubbed it. Now we're just waiting for the water to boil."

"You cook it live?"

"Yeah."

"That seems cruel."

"It's the only way I've ever seen it done," Chris said. "It's how the great chefs cook them in the best restaurants. And the crustaceans' ability to feel pain is up for debate. As human beings we tend to humanize all organisms when, in fact, a lobster has no central nervous system and therefore no ability to process a thought, or any sense of pain.

On the flip side, some studies have suggested that even low-level organisms react negatively to certain stimuli, so maybe they do feel something."

Oh.

Chris was watching her, a small grin on his face.

"The water's boiling," she said.

"So it is." Turning, he picked up the lobster and held it above the pot. "We put it in headfirst because lobsters have a habit of whipping their tails, and you don't want it to splash boiling water all over you."

In a matter of seconds the crustacean was submerged. Chris put the lid on the pot. "It'll be ready to eat in ten minutes or so."

"How do you know when it's done?"

"When its shell is completely red and the meat is white with no translucency."

He looked so at home in the kitchen that Emma wanted to kiss him. She buried her head in the refrigerator instead. "I'd better get busy," she said, pulling out lettuce and cucumber, celery, onion and any other fresh vegetables she could find. She needed to occupy her hands. She had a fourth entry for her journal. *I want to have great sex with the man I marry.*

CHAPTER TWENTY-FOUR

DINNER WAS GOOD. The company was good. Too good. Once they'd finished their meal and cleared away the dishes, they relocated to the living room, ostensibly to choose a movie from Emma's extensive collection of DVDs to entertain them until bedtime.

Thinking he'd let her do the honors, Chris settled onto one end of the couch, and realized he wasn't quite finished with the last topic they'd been discussing. "You light up when you talk about your students," he said.

Emma sank onto the other end of the couch. "Really?" she said, a strange smile on her face. "I mean, I know that the classroom is where I need to be. I love teaching."

"And the girl you were talking about. The one whose uncle you don't trust. Does she ever call you like she says she will?"

"She hasn't, but I haven't seen any evidence that her uncle's actually done anything, either. His temper scares her. He throws things. But so far he hasn't hurt her. Still, she's a sensible girl and if she's afraid, there's probably cause. I've reported my concerns to the guidance counselor and principal at the school, and they've spoken with her mother. From there I can only hope and pray that she'll call me if anything happens."

"I don't think there were teachers like you when I was a kid."

"I'm sure there were. You probably just didn't ignite their protective instincts being the strong, self-sufficient guy you are."

He shifted, crossing his ankle over his knee.

"Yeah, well, from what I remember there were books to read, lectures, homework and tests. Period."

"Do you think you'd have stayed in school if you hadn't been bored?"

He hadn't said he'd been bored. "Maybe. Didn't make much sense to me to waste days sitting inside when I could be out making money."

"And your father agreed with you?"

"No. It was one of the few times he was truly disappointed in me. He threatened to keep me off the boat, but I gambled on the fact that I knew him better than that and quit, anyway. There wasn't anything he could do about it. I was sixteen."

"How long did he keep you off the boat?"

How did she know he'd gambled and lost? "Six months."

"And how old were you when you regretted your choice?"

"What are you, psychic?"

"Nooo. But I'm paid to be observant."

He quirked a smile at her. "I was twenty-three. And before you tell me what I did next…I got my GED followed by a Bachelor of Science degree with a major in business in night school. It took me nearly ten years."

Her eyes wide, she gaped at him. "You're kidding!"

"What, you didn't think a fisherman could be university-educated?"

"No, I guess I just didn't expect it. I mean, it's not like college was going to make you any better at what you do."

"It did, though. I doubled my income the first couple of years out of school through better management and record keeping. And by selling directly to the consumer. I met Don Carmine, the owner of Citadel's, when I was in school. He had this idea to open up a restaurant and have me supply his fresh lobster."

"Cody told me about that."

He nodded, and then said, "I was engaged once, too."

Her shock was palpable. "You were? I thought you were a confirmed bachelor!" She sounded almost accusing. Or hurt. As though he'd lied to her.

"So there's something about me you don't know. Sara is part of the reason I'm a confirmed bachelor," he said. "We met in high school. Growing up with a philandering mother, and a father who worked sixteen hours a day every day, I was a pretty serious kid. Sara made me laugh."

"You asked her to marry you because she made you laugh?"

"No. I asked her to marry me because she was my best friend. She still is a good friend—until you, she was my only real friend."

"Is she here in town?" Emma sounded interested. And something else, too. Something different.

But he knew better than to think that she could be jealous. It wasn't Emma's way. And they had no future together.

Shaking his head, he told her about Sara's husband, Jeff, their daughter, Lily, and their home in South Carolina.

"Sara broke off our engagement after a

pregnancy scare," he told her, making certain—just in case it had been jealousy he'd detected—that Emma knew without a doubt they could not have a future together. "I was horrified when she told me she was afraid she was pregnant. I was twenty-two. I didn't handle the situation very well. But the truth is, I feel the same way today as I did back then. The thought of having a child, of the responsibility that comes with it, the time and commitment kids take, does not sit well with me. I think of my childhood, of the times my father wasn't there, and I think how like him I am and…"

"It's okay, Chris. Don't worry so much."

The words—spoken for the umpteenth time—didn't ease his tension any.

"You got any other broken hearts out there?" she asked, her voice light. And her smile—her smile made him hungry all over again.

Which made him cantankerous. He had to stop this.

"Did you start your period today?"

"No."

"Aren't you getting the least bit worried about that?"

She met his gaze openly. "Not really."

His mother had been able to lie to him while looking him straight in the eye.

"How can you not be? You had unprotected sex and we know you have higher than normal levels of HCG in your system."

"I'm not late enough to worry," she said. "If it wasn't for your fears, I probably wouldn't even have called the doctor."

Her attitude was frustrating. Their whole lives were at stake and she wanted him not to worry?

"I've heard of women being in their fourth month of pregnancy without knowing they were pregnant. It's not like you get a memo sent up through your bloodstream."

"If I went four months without a period, I'd know."

Nothing she said calmed the panic growing inside him.

Chris felt a lot older than her all of a sudden.

"You were violently ill today. Even with the patch."

"I was seasick."

She'd pegged him right—intuited things that he hadn't told her about himself—but even people who were perceptive couldn't see themselves in an unbiased light.

And Emma wasn't giving him any indication that she was seeing this situation with any clarity at all.

"You had one of the worst cases of seasickness I've seen. It could have been a combination sickness."

Emma stood. "Look, Chris, if you want to drive yourself crazy worrying, then there's nothing I can do to stop you. But I'm not going to join you. I have plenty of real things to worry about right now."

"You know, don't you? You know whether or not you're pregnant."

"I told you all along that I don't think I am."

"Then let's go get another test. Take it tonight."

"We had a deal. I'm going for a blood test as soon as my doctor returns. There's no point in taking another home test. It's likely that the result will be the same. I haven't started my period so my HCG levels will still be high."

Was she evading the truth? Burying her head in the sand because she was afraid? As if hiding from it could change the facts.

He'd learned the art from his mother; women with something to hide were evasive.

"You wouldn't do something crazy like

plan to have my child without letting me know about it, would you?"

She whirled on him. "You're kidding, right?"

"I don't think you're being honest with me. I'm just trying to figure out why. By your own admission, your mother wouldn't be able to handle you dating a man from the docks so I'm doubly sure she'd have a problem with you being pregnant by one of us. It would be a repeat of her mistake, right? And, by your own admission, you do everything you can to keep your mother free from worry."

Shaking her head, Emma sighed and turned her back on him.

"I'm tired," she said, heading toward the stairs. "The bed in the spare room is made up. Please turn out the lights before you come up."

He could go after her. He didn't have much doubt that they would wind up having sex again.

"Emma?"

She paused on the third stair and looked at him over her shoulder. "Yeah?"

"I'm sorry. I'm just trying to understand."

"I have no proof that I'm pregnant, Chris. Or that I'm not. But I'm not getting worked up about it until I know. If I haven't been able to get in with my doctor by Tuesday, I'll take the home test again, just for you."

Fair enough. And damn him for doubting her. But who wouldn't, given the circumstances? Were the situation reversed he'd have taken the damned test several times a day.

But that was him. She was the one who was possibly pregnant.

"Did you lock the dead bolts?" He'd noticed the night before that all of her doors had dead-bolt locks that had to be locked and unlocked with a key, even from the inside.

She'd carried the key up to bed with her. "Yes."

Which meant that if he suddenly needed a beer from the store, or a walk to clear his mind, he'd have to go into her bedroom to retrieve the key.

And if he did that, he'd never make it out.

ROB CALLED AGAIN late that night. Emma pushed the end button after the first half ring.

And less than a minute later, a nude and far-too tempting Chris appeared in her bedroom doorway.

"Don't you ever wear clothes to bed?" she asked.

"No." He was frowning. "Who called?"

"Rob."

"Did he leave a message?"

Just as he finished the question her phone signaled a new voice mail. "Right here," she said, holding up the phone.

With no apparent self-consciousness, Chris came into the room and over to where Emma had been sitting up in bed with her journal.

"Let's hear it," he said.

Feeling far too vulnerable with her shoulders exposed and her breasts practically visible beneath the thin cotton of her nightgown, Emma concentrated on the keypad on her phone. She pushed the voice-mail button and, when prompted, typed in her pass code.

"Hi, babe. Call me, please. Don't make me beg."

Just Rob. No threat. No aggressiveness.

"He's working on you. Trying to wear you down."

"He's not going to wear me down." She was too busy fighting Chris, and herself, to start thinking about the five years she'd spent with Rob or wondering if this sting operation was unfair to him.

He'd refused to cooperate when Miller and Hayes had called that first time after Cal's visit—when he'd had nothing at stake, and once she'd heard that, any influence Rob might have had on her was gone.

The Rob she'd known would have been happy to cooperate if it meant something he said might help them find Claire.

Still, she worried that she'd jumped on this sting operation as a way to legitimately spend a little more time with Chris before she said goodbye to him.

"You told Miller that he only calls once a day." Chris was still standing beside her bed. She could smell the musky scent of his aftershave.

"That's right, he did. Until today."

He shifted. Her gaze dropped to the dark hair on his thighs. "How many times has he called today?"

"This is the third time."

"When was the second?"

"Right after I came upstairs tonight."

"Did he leave a message that time?"

She wasn't reacting. "No, which is probably why he called back so soon."

"I don't like leaving you in here alone."

She didn't like being in there alone, either. And not because of any threat Rob might pose.

God help her, she was going to be a bad girl one more time.

CHAPTER TWENTY-FIVE

CHRIS DIDN'T LIKE GOING out on the water on Monday. For the first time in his life, he wished he could stay ashore.

The fact made him quake. Whatever had gotten into him had best get right back out. He was no knight in shining armor. Not for anyone.

Certainly not for a woman. They weren't to be trusted.

Standing aboard the *Son Catcher,* he froze on deck.

Women weren't to be trusted? Where in the hell had that thought come from? He'd trust Sara with his life. He trusted Marta. He trusted Emma Sanderson, too. But she was messing with his thoughts and that couldn't be tolerated.

Miller had said that in order to spur Rob into action they had to behave normally.

Emma was going to work today where there were security guards on the premises. And Miller's off-duty guys would be watching her—both of whom were more qualified to protect her than Chris was.

It wasn't his job.

Fishing was his job.

Squelching his urge to hunt down Rob Evert himself, Chris readied his bait, checked the boat to make certain there'd been no gas leaks or other mishaps overnight and set off to spend the day with the love of his life.

ROB CALLED EMMA on her way to work. And again halfway through first period. She always kept her phone on Mute during class, but she saw the call register on the screen. Ignoring the phone, she focused instead on her kids.

He'd called four times by lunch. And because she knew he knew she was in class, because he knew she couldn't answer, but was calling, anyway, Emma decided to listen to the messages he'd left.

All of them were exactly the same.

"Call me, babe. I need to speak with you."

The same words spoken with the same intonation. Every single time. It was weird. Unsettling. Was Rob losing his mind?

Or deliberately playing with hers?

Looking over her shoulder as she walked through a hallway swarming with teenagers on their way to class or to second lunch period, she wished she could speak with Chris. Let him know what was going on. She wanted to hear his voice.

But Chris was unavailable. He was out on the ocean, inaccessible.

As he would always be—no matter what the emergency.

Forgoing lunch, Emma slipped into her principal's empty office and dialed Detective Miller.

"Did you save the messages?" His no-nonsense tone didn't make her feel any more comforted.

"Yes."

"Forward them to me, as soon as we hang up."

Students were milling about in the foyer outside the office. Things were normal. Safe. "Okay."

"And don't go anywhere alone."

"I live alone."

"You'll be at work for several hours yet, correct?"

"Yeah. I'm done at four."

"Don't leave there until I get back to you."

"You're scaring me, Detective."

"Good. Until we have a better understanding of what's going on with this guy, I want you scared. I want you alert and watching out for yourself. I want to make certain you don't underestimate this guy just because you used to be in a relationship with him."

"Point taken, Detective," she said.

"You'll be hearing from me."

What she heard was a click in her ear as the man hung up.

ALTHOUGH SHE WANTED to bury her cell phone in the bottom of her purse for the rest of the day and focus on teaching, Emma kept the phone on her desk.

She saw the flash when Rob called during fifth period. And again between sixth and seventh periods. She saw the notification that she had two new voice mails.

And toward the end of her last period, she saw Lucy Hayes's number flash on her screen.

"Everyone take the last few minutes to get started on your journal entry for the week," she told her class. "Remember, this week, you're Abe Lincoln. Tell me what you're thinking. I'll be just outside the door, so don't get any wise ideas." She never left her students in class alone. Ever.

"Ms. Sanderson?" Jamaal Wayley called out.

"Yes, Jamaal?" She faced the tall, starpoint guard on the school's basketball team who was an even better writer than he was an athlete.

"We can write about anything, right? Doesn't have to be about politics or things that really happened while he was president?"

Which meant she might get an imagined trip to a strip club.

"Keep it clean, Jamaal. You know the rules. Nothing X-rated. You have to be Honest Abe."

He was baiting her. She knew it. And he knew she knew it. She also knew his entry would be the best one she'd get that week. The kid had talent.

By the time she made it to the hall, she'd missed Lucy's call, but luckily the detective picked right up when she called her back.

"Detective Miller said you were done at four," Lucy said. "Are you someplace you can talk?"

"Class actually ends at five after four." Emma's heart started to pound. If they were calling her on the dot of four, then this was serious. "I'll have the classroom to myself in about fifteen minutes. Detective Miller asked me to stay put until I heard from him."

"I told him I'd call you," Lucy said. "Fifteen minutes, you said? I'll sit right here by my phone until I hear back from you."

Walking slowly back into her classroom, Emma barely noticed the twenty-two restless teenagers who were shoving things into backpacks and chattering to one another as the bell rang, setting them free.

She wanted them out of there. She wanted them safe.

She needed to talk to Chris.

"First, Ramsey spoke with your friend Chris. He agreed to continue with the relationship plan for another day or two, at least," Lucy said as soon as she picked up Emma's ring. "He said he'd meet you at your place at six, if that's okay with you."

Chris was back onshore, then? Accessible?

"That's fine." It wasn't. At all. The good mood that had suddenly settled on her was the final straw. She had to get Chris Talbot out of her life. Her problems were not his. She wouldn't have his life in danger. She intended to tell him so just as soon as she saw him that evening.

"Until then, Ramsey wants you to keep up your daily routine as much as possible without making yourself a target."

"What does that mean, exactly?"

"Don't go anywhere alone where you're easily accessible."

"The school's going to be deserted, except for the nighttime cleaning crew, in about an hour," she said aloud. "I can go to my mother's. That's something Rob would find completely normal."

"Fine. Chris said he'd call you when he's on his way over. The two of you can arrange to meet at your place. In the meantime, Detective Miller got the okay to keep our guys on you for another couple of days."

"Seems like an awful lot of bother and expense because a guy refuses to take no for an answer. This kind of stuff happens all the time, and I've never heard of a woman getting police protection over it. The most I've ever heard of is someone getting a restraining order."

This case wasn't that simple. She knew that. But...

"It's understandable if you're getting cold feet, Emma. You have the right to end this at any time. We can pull Chris out of there, too."

"And then what?"

"Then we figure out another way to go at this. I have to be honest with you, though. There's something going on here and Detective Miller feels—and I agree with him—that we'd be remiss to drop this."

"Then I'm in. One hundred percent." She paused. "How often is Detective Miller right about his hunches?"

"Often enough that his captain pretty much gives him the green light any time he has one."

Fear had been her constant companion for twenty-five years. Emma was beginning to doubt that she'd ever be free. She'd taken some crazy chances lately and was more afraid than ever.

"Okay, tell me what you want and I'll do it."

"Just continue what you're doing," Lucy told her. "Go about your business as normally as possible. And stay in touch with us. Based on the escalating number of calls you've been receiving, we think the plan is working. Evert's getting more nervous. Chances are he'll show his hand soon."

"Maybe I should talk to him."

"We may get to that, but Ramsey doesn't think it's time yet."

"Did you find a connection between Rob and my sister's case?"

"No. So far we've all come up blank. I'm not at liberty to disclose exactly what we're doing but if there was a connection we'd find it."

"And you still think Claire was in Aurora?"

"Her DNA was on a couple of items removed from the nursery in that house. But it's always possible that those items came from somewhere else."

She nodded.

"We might not ever know when or why. One thing is for sure, we're talking about DNA that was left there more than eight years ago because the place was cordoned off as a crime scene, and then torn down after that."

"Do you think she could still be in Aurora?"

"Anything's possible, but not one other baby that passed through that home stayed in Aurora. Very few were even in the state of Indiana for any length of time. That was part of the reason the business ran so successfully for so long. In most cases, the woman didn't hold on to the children for more than twenty-four hours. She had a prescreened database of potential parents who were all willing and prepared to collect their new baby with only a few hours' notice. They were also only interested in newborns. None of them wanted to deal with children who might have memories that could get them caught, or who would miss the parents left behind."

Emma understood. And struggled to accept what she was hearing. "But she was there—or at least associated with someone else who was."

"Our theory is that whoever took Claire knew about the Aurora operation. As we've told you, the woman did business all over the East Coast and Midwest. She had more than one Massachusetts baby. Claire's kidnapper most likely knew about the Aurora business and tried to sell her to this woman but was turned down because of Claire's age."

And the detective had already evaded Emma's earlier attempt to find out what Lucy thought would have happened to Claire at that point.

"Let's concentrate on what we've got," Lucy said. "On finding out what Rob wants and whether or not there's a connection between him and the missing evidence. There's always a way in to the answers, Emma, we just have to find it."

"But what if the clues are buried so deep that they've been lost forever?"

"We have patience. And we keep looking."

"And sometimes you die before finding the answers, right?"

"There are unsolved cold cases in our vault that date back more than seventy years."

"Rob's a perfectionist. If he makes a mistake, it won't be an obvious one."

"No one's infallible. We haven't been able to link him to Claire yet, but we did come up with something. Do you know someone named Cheryl Diamond?"

"No. Why?"

"You're sure? You've never heard the name? Seen it anywhere? Heard it mentioned?"

"I'm sure. Who is she?"

"Someone who works as a clerk in the Comfort Cove traffic division."

"Would she have access to evidence rooms?"

"Not generally, but with a badge that lets her into the station house, she'd have a better chance of getting into the evidence vault than someone off the streets."

"You think Rob knows her?"

"She hangs out in online chat rooms where men go to have internet sex. We think Rob met her there. We have reason to believe that they've been…familiar…for several years. I can't say a lot, but there's some webcam evidence that our computer specialist uncovered. Ramsey's talked to Cheryl, but at this point she's denying even knowing about the existence of the chat room. Rob denies knowing her. We don't have enough yet to bring either of them in. At this point, you're still our only real way to get your ex-fiancé."

"Okay. I'll do whatever it takes."

"It could get dangerous. You need to understand that."

"I understand. I'll do anything to help solve the mystery of my sister's disappearance. I don't like involving Chris, though."

"Ramsey was pretty straight with him. He gave him every chance to duck out. The guy's insisting on following this through."

Because he thought she was pregnant with his child?

If she'd just start her damned period this could all end.

She'd called the doctor's office again that morning. The earliest she could get in was Wednesday. Which meant that tomorrow night she was going to have to take another one of those damned home pregnancy tests. Which would show the same elevated hormone levels because her stupid cycle was off, and then Chris would really start to panic.

And what? Ask her to have an abortion?

Which, of course, she would never do.

Or, maybe he'd sign off on his paternity?

Which would be fine. Better for her and the baby.

If there even was a baby.

Which there wasn't.

"I think Chris likes you," Lucy was saying before Emma had caught on to where the other woman was going with the conversation.

"We're more than a decade apart in age." The statement was weak. "And complete opposites."

"Opposites attract."

Emma told the detective about her father. And Chris's own dedication to a life on the ocean.

"I'm sorry, Emma." The sincerity in Lucy's words almost broke her. "I misunderstood. I thought maybe you and Chris were starting something. I shouldn't have pushed. Hopefully we'll get through this quickly and you'll be able to move on and meet someone who will make you as happy as you deserve to be."

People didn't always get what they deserved. Claire had certainly not deserved to be stolen from her family. Rose had not deserved to lose the child she'd paid such a high price to bear.

And look at Lucy...

"What about you and Ramsey Miller?" she asked. "You two seem pretty close."

"We think the same, professionally speaking."

"You spend a lot of time together."

"Not really. Last week was only the second time we'd ever met. We talk on the phone. Mostly about work. Ramsey's married to the job, Emma. Truth be told, I'm not sure he has it in him to open up to intimacy. Some people are just that way."

"Something must have happened in his past. Something that made him this way."

"I'm sure you're right. But it's not just Ramsey. I love my job, too. Way more than I can ever see myself loving a man. Any man."

"Don't you want a family of your own someday? Kids?"

"Truthfully? I'm not sure. With the things I see on the job…this job does something to you. It takes away your innocence. Once you've crossed a line, once you know things, once you've seen firsthand things that no one should have to see, you can't go back. A normal life in suburbia doesn't work for you anymore. It's not real."

Maybe that was Emma's problem, too. Not the seeing part, but the knowing. Maybe she couldn't believe in real happiness because she knew how quickly it could be taken away. Maybe she'd had it mostly right all along—

opting for safety and security over excitement and joy.

She'd just chosen the wrong man.

Twice.

CHAPTER TWENTY-SIX

CHRIS BROUGHT BACK ANOTHER lobster for dinner. Emma made garlic mashed potatoes and steamed asparagus.

If nothing else, they were both eating well.

"How is your mother?" Chris asked as they finished serving themselves.

"I didn't go to Mom's." Emma sat down and put her napkin in her lap.

Chris was a fisherman. He set his napkin, still folded, on one knee.

"I went to the Caffeine Café instead. Mom's getting ready to go to an educator's seminar on Wednesday and I didn't want her to see something different about me and do something stupid, like cancel," Emma said. She hadn't looked him in the eye since he'd gotten there. "She needs these times away. Four days to think about nothing except her job."

"You think she'd notice something different about you?" Like the fact that she was pregnant?

"I don't know, Chris." Emma's tone was truculent. It was a different side to her and he kind of liked it. "Let's see," she continued. "In the space of a few weeks I've slept with a man I didn't know, multiple times—"

"Well you only slept with him once when you didn't know him. Sleeping with a guy kind of qualifies as getting to know him, wouldn't you say?" Chris interrupted, feeling kind of irritable, himself.

"I've reunited with my stepbrother," she continued as though she hadn't heard him, "was told that my baby sister might have been a victim of a pedophile, then told she wasn't but that she was at a home known for black-market adoptions three states away. I caught my fiancé in bed with another woman, which Mom already knows, but now he's stalking me. I find out he has internet sex associations, and he probably has some connection to my sister's disappearance. I'm guessing someone as close to me as my mother would know that something's going on."

"You forgot to mention that you might be pregnant."

She shoved a hunk of lobster in her mouth, if a woman as refined as she could actually shove, the butter dripping down her chin.

He wanted to lick it off. She wiped her chin with her napkin.

"Yes, and even if I'm not, have someone making sure I worry about it. So if that's why you're here, because you think you have to be in case I'm carrying your child, you can go now."

"You're telling me to leave?"

"Would it do any good if I was?"

"No."

"But you admit that you're here because you think I might be pregnant."

"I'm here because I'm not a man who can walk out after giving my word, or my commitment, to anything."

Which was why he would never marry. Never have a family. He knew he could not be true to the commitment.

"If I walked out and Evert got away with this and hurt you, or anyone else...well, let's just say I need to be able to look myself in the mirror."

"I don't think he's physically dangerous."

"I'm not willing to take that chance. And obviously, neither are the off-duty police officers keeping a watch on you. Besides, if Evert's somehow involved in your sister's disappearance, if keeping up this charade can help you and your mother find some answers, then I want to help. No one should have to live with what the two of you have been through these past twenty-five years."

He'd said more than he meant to, but the words must have mollified her as she finished her dinner without another word.

And before the tension building in both of them had another chance to explode, Chris took Emma upstairs to bed. It was going to be the last time he'd have sex with her. It had to be.

INCONCLUSIVE AGAIN.

Emma wasn't surprised at the results of the pregnancy test Chris had handed her when he'd walked in the door Tuesday evening after work. She'd been hoping that with everything else that was going on he'd have been able to let it go another day—her doctor's appointment was tomorrow.

"I told you this might happen. My cycle is about to begin again. The internet said that can sometimes cause higher than normal levels of HCG, just not enough to confirm pregnancy."

He was standing before her in black jeans, a black T-shirt and the blackest expression she'd ever seen on his face.

"Don't you think that if I was pregnant, the

HCG should have risen enough in a week's time to change the results?"

"You have an appointment with your doctor tomorrow, right?"

"Yes." The man was beside himself. Emma's heart reached out to him. Putting the test kit in the trash, she turned off her bathroom light and led the way downstairs.

"Let's watch a movie. Get your mind off things."

"Will she give you an answer the same day?"

"Chris…" She knelt by the DVD shelf to the right of the large flat-screen television Rob had insisted they get. "Try to relax."

He stood over her.

The man was desperately afraid of the thought of being a father. If she'd needed any more proof that he was wrong for her, he was serving it to her on a silver platter.

"Yes, she'll give me an answer before I leave the office. There's a lab on-site and that kind of test doesn't take long for results." Giving up on the movie, she took his hand and pulled him over to the couch. Rob had called seven times that day and left the same brief message.

And, so far, besides making the phone

calls, he'd done nothing out of the ordinary since Miller had begun looking at him.

"Maybe we should go out. Have a glass of wine or something," Emma said.

"You shouldn't. Not until we know for sure you aren't pregnant."

"Fine. I'll have tea."

"You really aren't worried at all?"

"No, I'm really not." At least, not that she'd ever admit. If she found out she was wrong, that she was somehow carrying Chris's child inside her, she'd have plenty of time to panic then.

"What's the point?" she said. Maybe she could help him see that his way of dealing with this was counterproductive. "It's like borrowing trouble. It's not as though I can do anything at this point to reverse what happened. If I could go back in time I would. If I have to pay for my negligence sometime in the future, I will. But right now, I don't feel pregnant and I'm going to save myself the stress of worrying about it. Life's too short and gives you enough trouble to borrow more." Emma was so concerned about kidnappers, Claire's fate and a dangerous ex-fiancé, that the possibility of an unplanned pregnancy just didn't seem that threatening at the moment. The whole idea seemed surreal.

He seemed to ponder her words and Emma went back to browsing her movie selection. Anything that would take her mind off Claire. And Rob. And the fact that she and Chris were so diametrically opposed.

The real tragedies.

CHRIS WAS FEELING cantankerous. He'd had more sex in the past week than he'd had in one week's time ever. And he was randy again.

And worried, damn it. He'd always heard that stress wreaked havoc on a guy's libido. He wasn't seeing it. The woman of his desires was thumbing through movies as though she didn't have a care in the world. From where he sat, she had more to deal with than he would've been able to handle. "What *do* you worry about?"

"You want the truth?" She stared at him.

He wasn't sure how to answer that. Of course he wanted the truth. But he didn't want to know her any better. "Yeah," he said finally.

"What I'm most worried about these days, what I worry about almost constantly, is the fact that all I have to do is look at you and I'm suddenly willing to risk anything just to feel you inside me one more time."

He shouldn't have asked. His zipper was ready to burst.

"I'm like a stranger to myself when you're around," Emma said. "I hate it."

He didn't. But he should.

"I don't know what it is about you, but you're a lethal weapon and I can't seem to keep myself out of the line of fire."

He had to stop her.

"And what if this is it for me?" she added. "I've never reacted like this to a man before. What if I never do again?"

"You will." He found his voice. He was older, so supposedly wiser. It was up to him to steer them both out of danger. "Trust me on that one. Sexual attraction is merely a set of circumstances."

"You're saying sex feels just as good for you all the time?"

"No, but our circumstances—"

"Do you feel turned on all the time when we're together?" she interrupted, her eyes burning right through him.

"No." He was his mother's son, apparently, able to lie while looking someone in the eye. "When we have sex, yeah, I get turned on. But that's normal."

"That's it? You only get turned on when

we're intimate? So, it has nothing to do with me, in particular?"

"That's right." He was doing her a favor.

"I'm disappointed in you, Chris."

So be it. It was for the best.

"I'm just telling it like it is," he said, sealing their fate. Relief was good. He'd concentrate on that.

And hope to ignore, and forget, the pain he saw in her beautifully expressive brown eyes.

"No. If what you just said was true and you really were telling it like it is, I'd be embarrassed—humiliated, even—but I wouldn't be disappointed. I didn't figure you for a man who would lie to me. That's what disappoints me."

Shit. Chris sat up. "I don't lie." The words came from deep within. From the boy who'd adored a woman who wouldn't be straight with him. From the man who swore to himself that he would never be like her.

"You did just lie," Emma said. "You were as hard as a board a few minutes ago. You're definitely aroused by me—and not just when we're having sex. I'm not alone here."

Chris sat back. Wiped his hand over his face, and then laughed. "Aw, Emma, what the hell am I supposed to do? Yeah, you turn me on. All the time. But I've lived four decades, have four decades' worth of experiences that have given me wisdom, and I know that you and I are a recipe for disaster. Everything you want and need, physical attraction aside, is the exact opposite of what I want and need—or even have the ability to give to you."

"I know that."

"So I thought I was doing us both a favor by shutting this down. It's going to end, anyway. Tomorrow. Or the next day. Or soon after that. But with us spending this time together, we're getting to know each other better and better, and someone's going to end up hurt. We probably both will."

"I know." Her voice sounded strong. "I'm as determined as you are to end this, Chris. I just don't know how to stay away from you."

"Oh, Lord, woman, I can't seem to keep my hands off you, either." Chris reached for her, pulling her on top of him and plunging his tongue deep inside her mouth.

And heard someone coming down the stairs.

CHAPTER TWENTY-SEVEN

EMMA HEARD THE FOOTSTEPS at the same time she felt herself spin over and be crushed. She couldn't breathe. Chris's body held her down to the cushions. His lips pressed against her cheek, blocking her head from view.

In the second it took her head to clear, she realized he was protecting her.

"Let her up, Talbot."

Rob's voice! How had he gotten in her house? She'd had the locks changed. No one but her mother had a key. The windows were all dead-bolted from the inside. She'd double-checked them on Saturday after her meeting with the detectives.

"How'd you get in?" She gasped for air, her words muffled behind Chris's shoulder.

He held up a single key. "With this, of course. I was upstairs getting some discs I needed for work when I heard you both come in. Nice little scene there in the bathroom. I was just around the corner in the office, waiting with bated breath. So you think you're knocked up? No problem. We'll say the baby's mine."

The off-duty cops were protecting *her,* watching *her,* not her house. Regular-duty officers were making random drive-bys on her house. It would have been easy enough for Rob to watch for police cars and slip into the backyard when the coast was clear.

And then it dawned on her.

He had her mother's key. He'd gotten to Rose.

"No!" she screamed, shoving her weight against Chris until she'd unbalanced him enough to get out from under him.

"What have you done to my mother?" she screeched at the man who was standing in the living room they'd shared for two years, a gun pointed at the man she'd been about to have sex with. Rob thought he'd pass Chris's baby off as his? Not in this lifetime.

Rob glanced at her, and then immediately back at Chris, the gun aimed straight at the older man's heart. "Rose is safe," he said, staring at Chris. He didn't so much as glance at Emma as he said, "I wouldn't hurt your mother. You should know that. I care about her."

"Put the gun down, Evert." Chris's voice.

In a tone Emma didn't recognize at all. It was deep. Threatening.

She was glad he was there.

And scared to death for him, too. If he died because of her—if he even got hurt because of her...

If something had happened to Rose...

"Like hell you care, Rob," she snapped. How could she ever have thought this man was safe? "Where is my mother?"

She couldn't live without Rose. Couldn't bear the thought of her mother afraid. In pain.

"She's apologized to the conference committee for her absence, and no one else is going to miss her for the next few days. Don't worry, she's perfectly safe." His smugness nauseated her.

Emma took a step toward him. "Where is Rose?" she yelled. "What have you done with her?" She had to keep him talking.

She had to get to her mother. Assuming Rose was still alive.

She was.

Emma had to believe that.

"Let's just say she won't be making any phone calls anytime soon," Rob said, turning her blood cold. "Maybe never unless you come with me."

"She's not going anywhere with you,"

Chris said, putting himself in front of Emma. "You're not going to get away with this."

"Step aside, old man. You had your chance to do what was best for Emma, but you were more interested in getting in her pants. You don't care for her at all."

"Put the gun down." Chris moved toward him.

"Stop or I'll shoot." With both hands on the gun now, Rob kept a steady aim on Chris's chest.

"Don't, Rob! Stop this craziness! Tell me what you want from me."

"It's a little late for that now, Em. I've been trying for weeks to tell you what I want, but you've ignored all my calls. To be fair, I gave you lots of chances. All of this could have been avoided if you'd only called me back."

This was all her fault? And Chris's for not listening to Rob's warning?

Thoughts flew through her mind. "I'm sorry," she said slowly, finding a calm that surprised her. "I should have called. I just needed time to figure things out."

"So what's Talbot here? Your *therapist?*"

"You can't really be angry with me for one indiscretion, Rob. Not after all the women you've slept with since we've been together. I was looking for a way to understand why you did what you did. Believe it or not, I was looking for a way to forgive you."

Rob stole a glance in her direction, his expression questioning.

Chris was moving slowly to the right, inching up on Rob. Emma kept talking.

"I couldn't forgive you this last time. Even after a few days passed, and the initial shock wore off, I wasn't okay. Before…was horrible. But now…with us engaged…you hurt me, Rob. Really bad."

His gaze was trained on Chris, the gun still held steady, but his jaw had loosened a bit.

"I had to do something." Emma kept the words coming. "You guessed it that Saturday after I met Chris," she continued. "You guessed that I'd spent the night with someone. You said you were relieved, remember?"

"Sleeping with him is one thing, but seeing him? Like you're a couple? Having him in your home, like he could move in, be a part of your life, that's unacceptable."

And this man with the red, twisted face was not Rob.

She couldn't look at Chris. Couldn't draw attention to him. But she wanted to.

"You brought Tiffany into our bed, Rob. Remember? That was a first. And that was why it was so hard for me to get over it this time. Besides, as you now know, I'm afraid I'm pregnant."

Were Miller's off-duty officers outside? Rob had been in the house since before she and Chris got home—and he'd entered with a key—so there was no obvious sign anything was amiss.

How did she alert them?

She'd yet to see one of them. She didn't know if they were watching her 24/7 or in shifts. She hadn't thought to ask.

Hadn't really wanted to know.

Hadn't wanted to believe she'd need them.

And what about the random drive-bys from the duty officers? Would anyone notice she and Chris were in trouble?

"Tell me what I have to do to get my Mom back," she said, not daring to plead for Chris's safety, as well. But she prayed for it.

"You're going to come with me," Rob said. "I knew if I couldn't get you to talk to me, all I had to do was get to Rose. You'd do anything for that woman." Rob's voice dripped disgust. "You act like her life is more valuable than yours. It's your fault that people shit on you, Emma. You let them. But I'm not like you. I don't let people shit on me. Not even you."

"What have I done to you?" Instinctively

Emma moved forward, toward Rob, toward his gun, with some idea that she'd get his attention away from Chris, if nothing else.

Rob didn't move the gun, but he looked at her. And Chris slid toward him from the side.

"You think after all the time I've put in, I'm going to let you throw me out like yesterday's trash and bring someone else in here to reap the benefits?" Rob spat, spinning sideways to keep his gun aimed at Chris's chest.

The words were practically a repetition of what Rob had told Chris that day he'd threatened him by the dock.

"What benefits?" she asked, frowning with genuine confusion, praying that Chris would be safe.

"I don't even have a savings account, apart from my teacher's pension, and I can't cash in on that for another twenty years," she told Rob, drawing closer to him, trying to get him to look at her. "You know that."

"Don't play stupid with me, Emma. I've been telling you for years that you needed to reopen your sister's case. You know what this is about."

"About Claire? How do you benefit if we find Claire?"

Was Ramsey Miller right? Did Rob have ties to Claire's abductor? "If you know where my sister is, Rob, if you have any idea what happened to her, you'd better tell me now." She spoke through gritted teeth, feeling capable of grabbing the gun from the sanctimonious bastard and aiming it right at his face.

"I don't know where she is, but you can bet your life that someone does," Rob said. "Someone in the Comfort Cove Police Department. And now, you're going to come with me. We'll go get your mother, and the two of you are going to agree to keep quiet about all of this. You are going to marry me. Your mother is going to welcome me as her son-in-law. We are going to go on as planned, with one little difference. As soon as we're married, you and your mother are going to file a lawsuit against the city of Comfort Cove."

Emma took another step forward, making sure she didn't lose eye contact with Rob. "What for?"

"Negligence. You've got a seven-figure lawsuit sitting in your lap and you're going to cash it in."

A vague memory came back to her. When she and Rob were first dating, he'd told her about the class he'd taken in college that had dealt with liabilities. The class had been designed to keep students from falling prey to lawsuits. Rob had mentioned suing the city as a possibility in her sister's case, but after they'd talked she'd been certain they both knew there was no grounds.

"We don't have any proof of wrongdoing," she reminded him.

"Wrong again, Em. And from now on we're doing things my way. So first, because you've created a mess here, babe, you're going to take this gun and shoot our witness. You'll dispose of his body and this whole thing will be our little secret. And it will also be my insurance that for the rest of your life you're going to do exactly as I say or I will turn you in to the police for murder. You will never, ever ignore one of my phone calls again."

Chris lunged, but Rob got to her first, grabbing her by the neck. Rob had the advantage. Emma had planted herself right at his feet.

"Let her go, you bastard." There was venom in Chris's voice as he stood back, scowling at the gun Rob held pointed at his chest.

"Not on your life." Rob chuckled, tightening his hold around Emma's throat with the crook of his arm. "I'm just starting to enjoy myself." Keeping the gun trained on Chris, he brought the weapon close to Emma's hand

and hissed, "You're going to take this now, love. I'll help you keep the gun steady, but you are going to pull the trigger." He tightened his arm again and she choked, gasping for breath, and trying not to move at the same time for fear she'd make the gun go off.

Rob used the hand on the arm around Emma's throat, to pull her hand up and place it on the gun.

"Have you ever shot a gun before, Em?"

He knew she hadn't. He knew she was petrified of them. But she couldn't answer him, anyway. He wasn't leaving her enough air to speak.

She didn't have a lot of time before she lost consciousness. And she would not let it end this way. Not her life. Or Chris's. Or her mother's, either.

Her fingers were on the barrel of the gun. With his index finger, Rob forced her middle finger to the trigger. She was starting to see stars. Getting light-headed. She was going to faint.

But before she went down, she went limp beneath Rob's arm, becoming deadweight. She should have known he'd be prepared for the eventuality, that with his strength he could sustain her weight. But it didn't matter.

She wasn't afraid. Didn't feel any emotion at all as she felt her finger start to push against the trigger. She couldn't look at Chris, but his presence, the life she was saving, the joy she'd known with him, gave her strength.

She only had a second, that was all it took to jerk sideways, using every bit of strength she had to reposition the gun in the last second so that it was pointing at Rob.

Before she could succeed, she heard the explosion as the gun went off.

CHAPTER TWENTY-EIGHT

"Nooooo!" SEEING THE INTENT in Emma's eyes a fraction of a second before her arm moved, Chris lunged, bumping her hand just as the gun went off.

He fell, taking Emma and Rob and the gun with him.

She was not going to live with Evert's murder burdening her soul. And she wasn't going to die, either.

Rob reached for the gun, but Chris got to it first, just as Emma's front door burst open. "Police! Freeze!"

Two uniformed cops stood in the archway into the living room with guns pointing at them. They'd obviously heard the shot, alerting them that all was not well inside the townhome.

Rob still had an arm around Emma's throat. She lay still, but her eyes were wide open. She was blinking. Chris didn't see any blood.

"Drop the gun." The voice of the officer was menacing.

Not on his life. Keeping the barrel pointed at Rob Evert's head, Chris said, "Just as soon as you get him away from her," he said. "I'm Chris Talbot."

While one officer held a gun on Chris, the other moved in on Rob, prying him and Emma apart.

She coughed and bent over, and the officer helped her to a sitting position on the floor, his other hand holding Rob captive.

"We need to see some ID," the second officer said to Rob. While holding him up against the wall, he dug inside Rob's back pocket for a wallet. And then, not so gently, cuffed the man.

As soon as he heard the click, Chris surrendered Rob's gun and reached for Emma.

She might not need reassurance, but he did. He'd thought they were both going to die.

EMMA RODE WITH Detective Miller to her mother's place just after eight on Tuesday night. She'd refused the medical examination Ramsey had suggested she submit to and insisted that she needed to be with him at her mother's home, no matter what they found. Rob had been in custody for fifteen minutes, and, although she didn't know everything he'd told the detectives, she knew he was insisting that he hadn't done anything but visit with Rose.

Please, dear God, let this be one time he's telling the truth.

Rob had also claimed to have been in her home to pick up some discs he'd left in her office. He said he needed them for work.

When Miller had looked, the discs had been there, but Emma knew for certain that he'd brought them that evening. She'd made sure nothing of Rob's was left in the house after she'd kicked him out.

Rob maintained that Chris Talbot had been the one to threaten their lives that night. That he'd been pulling Emma away from Talbot when the gun went off.

There was a bullet hole in the wall near the window of her front room.

She had no idea where Chris was. He'd been ushered out of the living room by a couple of uniformed officers and she hadn't seen him since.

"You sure you won't let us run you by the hospital?" Detective Miller asked, sitting beside her in the backseat, while a female officer drove the unmarked car they were in.

The key to her mother's house clutched tightly in her hand, Emma shook her head.

The emergency room couldn't help her where she hurt.

She had to make certain that her mother was safe. She couldn't think beyond that.

"THE LIGHT'S NOT on in the corner of the living room," Emma said as they pulled up in front of what used to be a newish house in an up-and-coming neighborhood, but was now an older home in a below-average neighborhood.

"What does that mean?"

"She always turns that light on when she's leaving. She leaves others on, too, randomly, so there isn't a pattern, but she always leaves that light on in the corner so she can see the whole room when she walks in. My mother has an aversion to shadows."

"Is it ever on when she's home?"

"Yes."

Miller turned to look at her. "You see anything else amiss?"

"No. It looks perfectly normal. But if Rob took her, there probably wouldn't be much sign of struggle. It's not like he'd have to break in. My mother had no reason to fear Rob."

She should have told her mother what was going on.

Detective Miller opened his door. "Let's go in."

"If she's there, if everything is okay, will you let me tell her what's going on? Please? Mom doesn't do well with police officers. They weren't a huge help when Claire went missing. For months they treated her like she was a suspect."

"Stay in the car, would you, Brown?" The detective spoke to the officer in the front seat.

"Of course, sir. You want me to keep the car running?"

"Yeah."

THE MINUTE HE was told he was free to leave the police station, Chris sped back to his side of town. He made it to the *Son Catcher* without getting a ticket, and was on board with an open beer before he'd turned on any lights. He'd take the boat out, anchor her and make himself inaccessible for the rest of the night.

Evert was in custody.

Emma was safe.

For now, until she saw her doctor, he was free.

Tempted to throw his cell phone overboard, Chris held himself back.

He ran his business through his phone.

The satisfaction he'd gain from trashing it wouldn't be worth the cost of a new one.

"LET'S GO AROUND back." Emma—moving rapidly across the grass in her mother's front yard—wasn't giving the detective a chance to refute her.

"Mom!" she called as she unlocked the double-locked dead bolt into the kitchen. "I always call out to her so she'll know it's me," she explained to Miller.

"Emma? Who are you talking to? I thought you said you were having dinner with friends tonight." Rose's voice initially came from upstairs, but trailed downward. "I was going to call you later. You'll never guess who stopped by…"

Her mother, still wearing the tweed green dress and matching jacket that she'd probably worn to work that day, stopped in the doorway to the kitchen.

"Emma? What's going on? Who's this?"

Steeling the alarm from her voice, her expression, swallowing back tears of relief, Emma said, "Mom…"

"Is this the friend you were having dinner with, Em? As busy as you've been these past few weeks, I'd hoped you met someone, but then when Rob stopped by…"

Her mother was fine. Just fine.

And open to Emma bringing home a new boyfriend.

"I'm D—"

"Mom, he's not a friend," Emma interrupted, giving Miller a pointed look. "Can we sit down a minute?"

Rose paled. Her shoulders closed in on her. "What is it? You've got bad news. I know it. I can tell by the way your mouth is trembling. You're upset about something."

Her mother was filling the teakettle. Next she'd get out the cups. And saucers. She's put tea bags in each. She'd pull out a little plate and put some sweetened crackers on it.

"Tell me about Rob coming to see you," Emma said.

"First tell me who *he* is." Rose stared her down.

"He's a detective, Mom. Rob tried to hurt me tonight. He said that he'd taken you hostage and that if I didn't go with him he couldn't guarantee your safety."

Rose sank into the chair at the head of the small table. "And you believed him?"

"He had a key to my house, Mom. You have the only copy."

Shaking her head, looking dazed and frightened and reminiscent of the little girl she'd regressed into those first days after Claire went missing, Rose turned and pulled out the hidden drawer underneath the ledge of the butcher-block island. "My copy is right… He took it."

"Tell us about Rob Evert's visit, ma'am." Detective Miller pulled the saucers down from the cupboard, set the cups on them and placed them on the table before pulling out a chair and sitting opposite her mother. "If you don't mind, that is."

The teakettle whistled and Emma turned off the burner while Rose told them both about Rob's impromptu visit, repeating what must have been close to verbatim every word of the five-minute conversation that had taken place before he asked Rose if she wouldn't mind looking in her computer room for the discs he needed, in case he'd left them there.

"That must have been when he took the key," Emma said. Standing behind her mother, her hands resting lightly on Rose's shoulders, she looked at Miller. "He knew where it was."

"I assumed so. You ladies let him into your lives. Trusted him. He has a lot to answer for."

"Oh, no. Oh, no." Rose was trembling. "I left the room and he took the key and… I put you in danger, Em. I can't believe it. I put you in danger. I'm so sorry. I—"

"As you can see, your daughter's fine, Mrs. Sanderson," Detective Miller said in a voice Emma hadn't heard before. "You taught her to take care of herself well."

"You saved yourself, Em?"

From Rob? Yeah, she'd found a way to get out of giving in to his demands. But she'd have ended up a murderer if not for...

"Yeah," she said now. If she'd hurt Rob, killed him, it would have been self-defense. She knew that. But earthly laws didn't make her feel as though taking a life was okay.

"She outsmarted him," Miller said, and Emma gave him a warning look.

Rose stared and Emma forced herself to erase any trace of the past few hours from her face.

"You're really fine?" Rose asked.

"Yes, Mom, I'm fine." Rob was in custody. Chris was gone. And she wasn't concerned about being pregnant. Claire was still missing, there were no further answers in her case, but that was normal for them.

"Where's Rob?"

"In jail," Detective Miller said. "Where I hope he's going to be for a very long time."

"Even though he didn't hurt her?"

"He was in her house when she got home tonight. He held her there against her will, which is considered kidnapping. He threatened bodily harm and he attempted to blackmail her. All serious felonies punishable by twenty years or more in prison."

If they could prove any of it, Emma thought. She was sure Rob would try to turn it into a case of her word against his. Rose said he could take the key. Emma said he was welcome to his discs. Both statements were true, but in a different time and under different circumstances.

Which they had no way to prove.

And between Rob and Chris? Chris was the one with the gun when the officers burst into the room. And he'd refused to relinquish it at first.

Hopefully the Cheryl Diamond thing was going to pan out.

Or they'd find out what Rob was really up to before it was too late.

"YOU'RE GOING TO come clean with me." Ramsey Miller stood over Evert, who was sitting, hands cuffed in his lap, at a table in the interrogation room Tuesday night.

"I don't know what you're talking about."

He tossed a picture of Cheryl Diamond

in front of the man. "She gave you up, man. She's talking. Now's your chance to have your say before we agree to the deal she's asking for."

"I've never seen that girl before in my life. If she thinks she has something on me, I'm willing to take my chances."

"You're already going away for a long time, you get that, don't you?"

"For what? Defending myself from my ex-fiancée's jealous lover? You heard your guys. When they burst in, Talbot had a gun on me."

"Uh-huh, and you just happened to stop by for...what? A friendly chat?"

"I came by to get some discs I forgot in Emma's office. I needed them for work. She's given me a key."

Evert was not changing his story. At all.

Because it was well rehearsed? Or the truth?

"What about Rose Sanderson?"

"What about her? Last I saw her, she was fine."

"You admit to seeing her, then?"

"I did see her, briefly, yes. This afternoon. I stopped by her place to see if she could help me iron things out with Emma. We talked for a few minutes, and when I could see she wasn't going to be much help, I asked her if she minded if I look for the discs that I later found at Emma's. She looked for me, said she didn't have them, and when she said she thought it was best that I leave, I did. I'm sure she'll verify that."

"Emma says that you claimed to have forced Rose to call the organizers of the conference she was supposed to attend and say she wasn't coming."

"Emma says a lot of things that aren't exactly true, but that's a stretch, even for her. All those years, growing up with a mother like hers, always having to look over her shoulder, never trusting anyone, being afraid, it's all taken its toll on her."

The lowlife was twisting the truth into lies, but Miller wasn't done with him yet.

CHAPTER TWENTY-NINE

EMMA WAS AT HER doctor's as soon as the office opened Wednesday morning. She was only five minutes from school and had plenty of time before she had to be in her classroom. She'd learned a long time ago that the best way to survive tragedy was to go on. To find normal again.

"The doctor's not here yet, but we can get the blood work done so the results will be ready when she arrives," the receptionist, a new woman she'd never met before, told her. "Because you're one of our patients, the test is free of charge."

She already knew that, and couldn't care less about the money. Not that she bothered explaining either point to the poor woman behind the desk. It wasn't her fault the mere thought of Chris Talbot—the man who hadn't called her at all last night, hadn't picked up when she'd called him—made her tense enough to snap.

"My appointment with the doctor isn't

until four-thirty, but she'd suggested that I get the lab work done this morning," she told the receptionist, forcing herself to smile in hopes that the expression somehow translated into her voice.

"Of course." The woman called for Christine, a nurse that Emma knew by sight, and the whole thing was over in a matter of minutes.

By five o'clock that afternoon, she'd be free of her last tie with Chris Talbot. She hoped. And then felt like crying again.

Minutes later, Emma pulled into the teacher's parking lot at school, found a space and picked up her phone, calling up the notepad feature.

Detective Miller had suggested that she should take the day off work. Maybe see a counselor. He'd offered to set her up with one.

After all, she'd been involved in an attempted murder the night before.

Chris's. Miller didn't know Emma had tried to turn the gun on Rob, instead.

He also didn't get that her job was what kept her sane. Not counseling. She'd had enough of that over the years.

She'd go into school. She'd do her job.

And then she'd do the last thing she was ever going to do for Chris Talbot.

She would set him free.

But first, she had another journal entry to make.

5. I want to have children.

As soon as he secured the *Son Catcher* for the night and sold his day's take to Manny, Chris left the docks. He went home, showered, put on fresh jeans, a black T-shirt and flip-flops, ran a comb through the wet hair tipping his shoulders and went straight back out to the truck.

It wasn't Friday. And it wasn't even dinnertime yet, but he pulled up outside of Marta and Jim's place and went to the door.

"Chris?" Marta had a worried smile on her face when she met him at the door. "Come in," she said, wiping her hands on her apron. "What's wrong?"

"Nothing's wrong."

"Jim's okay?"

"I haven't seen him today, Aunt Marta, but there wasn't anything out of the ordinary going on down at the docks. Did you expect him back early?"

"No." The older woman's grin lit up her

face. "I just…seeing you there, I thought—"
She sat down in her rocker. "No matter how
many years pass, I guess you never quite get
past the fear of…well, never mind."

He understood. "I'm sorry I frightened
you."

"No, it's fine. I just let my imagination get
away with me sometimes. So, tell me what's
up."

He didn't pretend this was just a social call.
If he'd made more of them in the past ten
years, maybe he could get away with it. But
what was the point?

"I need to talk to you, Aunt Marta. Have
you got a minute?"

"Just put the casserole in the oven. I've got
forty-five minutes before it's due to come
out."

"I need you to be completely honest with
me."

"I don't lie to you, son. I never have."

"I'm not accusing you of lying. I'm just
saying I need the complete truth."

"I'll do my best."

"Good. Then tell me about my mother."

"I knew Josie most of her life. What do
you want to know?"

"I want to know the things you don't talk
about. The things you've never told me."

"I don't want to speak ill of the dead, Chris. You know it's not right."

"I'm asking you to tell me the truth about my mother," he said again. "Besides the panic attacks. I think I have a right to know."

"Your mother was a good woman, Chris. She adored you and she adored your father."

He had cause to doubt her on both counts. Looking out at the ocean in the distance, he held his tongue. There was a right way and a wrong way. A phrase he'd heard his father say a million times.

"She...had problems."

An understatement. "She had men, you mean."

"You knew?"

"She didn't tell you about the day her twelve-year-old son walked in to find her naked in bed with a man he'd never seen before?"

Marta's head bowed. "No." Her eyes, when she looked back at Chris, were shadowed. "Chris, I didn't condone what your mother did."

"But you knew about it."

"Yes."

"You knew that she was being unfaithful to my father and yet, all those years, all those Friday nights, we'd sit here together like family and you never once told my father what you knew?"

"First, it wasn't my place to tell him about it."

"You and Jim were his best friends!" Chris stopped as his voice raised. "Who else should have told him something like that?"

"And secondly," Marta continued as though Chris hadn't spoken, "he didn't need to be told. He knew."

"Later, yeah, he found out somehow. But if he'd known from the beginning—"

"He knew fairly early on in their marriage."

The time when he was twelve wasn't the first? "You're sure about that?"

Marta nodded. "He talked to Jim about it."

"He did."

"He was heartbroken, of course, but he still loved your mother. And she loved him. She hated what she was as much as anyone. She begged your father, time and again, to forgive her, to not leave her."

"He should have left her."

"Maybe. Maybe not. It's not for us to say. Their relationship was between the two of them and who knows what was best for them."

Chris shook his head.

"Your mother grew up in a different time," Marta said. "You never knew her parents, but they were quite wealthy. Her father was a strict man who expected his wife and daughter to know their place and not to stray from it. In exchange they were pampered and spoiled and protected. There wasn't much money left by the time your grandmother died, but your maternal grandparents gave your house to your mom and dad as a wedding gift. Your mom loved being the boss of her own home, but she never learned how to be self-sufficient, how to rely on herself for anything. And each time she'd have a panic attack, she'd think she was going to die. She'd do anything to stop from having them. Being with...someone...stopped them."

Funny, for a woman who couldn't take care of herself, she'd certainly taught him how to.

"She was weak, Chris. She needed a man around to feel safe. And she fell in love with a man who couldn't be around."

She fell in love with the wrong man.

"I don't think she knew, when she first married your father, quite how isolated her life was going to be in that beautiful cottage on the hill. Her father had just died of a heart attack and her mother had remarried and moved to Europe, and your dad had been great with her through all of that. She was so in love with him. She found him exciting and different from anything she'd ever known. Where her father stifled her, your father gave her freedom. It seemed as though they were great for each other.

"It didn't hit her how completely alone she was until she went into labor with you. Your dad was out to sea and there was no way to reach him. She was in so much pain and petrified. You came very quickly and she hemorrhaged, and she had to face that all alone."

It was the challenging times in life that shaped you, that provided you with the opportunities to make the choices that defined who you were. More sage words from his father.

"By the time your father got there, it was all over, but she didn't ever seem to get past that feeling of being alone and helpless. She started to obsess about your father being gone, about something happening while he was out at sea. Her father had taught her that she couldn't do things on her own."

Chris didn't want to understand. It was easier to blame her.

"Your dad didn't take a single day off when you were born, or at any other time, either. When you had colic, had your tonsils out, played your first T-ball game. The sea beckoned to him, just like it does Jim and you and Trick and the others. He had a family to support and the ocean was his sole provider."

She didn't have to explain that part to him.

"He wasn't there for many of the important moments, Chris. He missed not only your first steps and first words, but the time you fell and hit your head and had to have stitches...the time you had rheumatic fever...."

Marta's voice trailed off, but Chris didn't need her to remind him of all the times he'd needed his old man and hadn't had him there. He knew better than Marta all the things his father had missed. Baseball games. Science projects. Father-son campouts.

"I used to think that your father stayed because of you. He wanted to raise you. He worried about what kind of life you'd have if your mother took you to live with her someplace else."

"With her whoring around, he could have sued for custody."

"You were a baby, Chris. Back then, they didn't take babies from their mothers. Besides, she was a good mother. A really good mother. She put you first in everything she did. No one could doubt how much she loved you."

A flash of memory surfaced. His mother, beautiful in a dress that came in at the waist and then flowed out around her, was smiling at him. He wasn't sure why. He'd loved her so much. The memory faded.

"Later, I understood that your father stayed with her because he loved her too much to let her go. And because she loved him. It's hard to understand. Lord knows I spent years trying. I was the one she'd come to after she'd been with another man. She'd cry so hard I thought her ribs would break. She hated herself. For a time, she talked about suicide. I went with her to counseling. But nothing was stronger than her need to feel safe. Secure. Cared for. Her affairs were short-lived. Far between. And discreet. Your father made up his mind that they weren't worth losing her over."

"Until she decided to divorce him."

"She was older then. More mature. She'd accepted who she was. You were grown and out on the water, too. It was obvious you'd chosen to follow your father's way of life. And she couldn't face growing old alone. She'd gotten to the point where she dreaded getting up every morning to face another day. She was afraid something would happen to her and no one would know. She was forgetting things and was afraid she'd lose her mind. She asked your father to turn the boat over to you and give her the rest of his life, but he couldn't do it. He came over here. Talked to Jim about it at length, but he just couldn't leave the sea. He knew he'd be no good for either of them.

"For what it's worth, I don't think she'd have gone through with the divorce." Marta started to rock, staring out at the water that ruled all of their lives. "She loved him too much."

A love story doomed from the beginning.

"She didn't lie to him." He let the revelation sink in. Those times he'd known his father had known, the times his father had come home and treated his mother as though nothing was amiss—his father hadn't been living with a lie, he'd just been living with an unfaithful spouse.

An openly unfaithful spouse.

"No, Chris. Your mother never lied to your father. She didn't hide things from him, either. The very first time she was with another man, she told your father right away. She was so ashamed."

He nodded. Thought about the vagaries of life.

One thing was for sure. He was not going to make the same mistakes his parents had made. Men like him and his father were not meant to marry.

"It must have been hard on you and Jim, knowing what was going on, not being able to do anything to help."

"It was."

He turned his head. "And what about you, Aunt Marta? How did you cope all these years with Jim out there?" He motioned to the water.

"It wasn't easy, son, but it was probably easier because I didn't have children. I wasn't bearing that responsibility alone like your mother was. I was lonely a good chunk of the time. It probably would have been better if I'd had a job. But I got involved with the other wives, got involved in the politics of lobstering, made myself a part of our family's business as best I could. I was better at being alone than your mother was.

"And sometimes Jim and I had hellacious fights."

It was getting dark. Jim would be home soon. He could smell Marta's casserole.

It was time to go.

EMMA CALLED CHRIS. Twice. He wasn't picking up. And her news shouldn't be left as a message. But she wasn't going to drive out to the docks. Not at night. By herself.

Not ever. She couldn't see Chris again.

She had one more conversation to have with him and then their connection would be severed.

She went home. Made some tea. Drew a hot bath. And prayed that when she got out she'd be ready to tackle the rest of her life.

CHAPTER THIRTY

THE FIRST THING CHRIS DID when he got back in his truck was check his phone. Her doctor's appointment had been at four-thirty.

He couldn't move on until he knew for sure that he and Emma Sanderson had not made a baby together.

Adrenaline pumped through him when he saw two missed calls. Both from her.

He pushed a button to return the call, and then just as quickly, his thumb hit the end-call button. She'd called twice. Which bespoke urgency.

Meaning her answer was that she was pregnant? Or was she just in a hurry to let him know he was free?

If she was pregnant he needed her to know that he would be there for her. That he was not going to desert her.

Or be shut out.

Not a message that could be imparted over the phone.

THE PHONE RANG while Emma was in the bath. She'd brought it in the room with her.

Chris's number flashed. And the call was lost.

Drying off, she put on a pair of cotton underwear that her mother had bought her for Christmas. A no-nonsense bra that she'd bought to give her extra support when she exercised. A T-shirt, baggy sweatpants and dark blue slipper socks completed her attire.

She needed a glass of chocolate milk. A glass and syrup in hand, she jumped when the phone rang again.

But she didn't procrastinate. She wanted to be brave enough to be fully alive. Journal entry number two in mind, she grabbed her phone, trying to ignore the fact that her hand was shaking.

She'd be fine. She always was.

"Emma? Lucy Hayes here. I hope it's not too late."

"Detective Hayes?" She hadn't even looked at the caller ID.

"Don't we know each other well enough to be on a first-name basis?"

"Yes, Lucy, sorry. I…" Stopping short of telling the detective who she'd thought she'd been about to speak with, Emma's mind went to Rob. "It's not too late," she said.

"I just got off the phone with Ramsey Miller," Lucy said. "We have some news, and I told him I'd give you a call."

Flipping off the kitchen light, Emma sank into a chair. "Okay."

"First, Cheryl Diamond came in today. Ramsey had already told her that Rob was in custody, hoping that she'd want to make a deal, but she'd denied knowing Rob. But computer-savvy woman that she is, she went on the Comfort Cove police public website, found Rob's booking record and when she saw the charges—when she realized she could be named an accomplice to kidnapping, blackmail and attempted murder—she decided to talk."

"Rob was charged with attempted murder?"

"He's being held on those counts, but charges are pending a grand-jury indictment."

"What about the fact that Chris was holding the gun when the police came in?"

"It was Rob's gun. He brought it to the scene, which incriminates him. And the officers testified that Rob had an arm locked around your throat on the floor when they burst in, and the marks on your neck supported that account.

"Chris was there at our request, as part of a department-approved sting, and he agreed to give up the gun as soon as Rob was in custody. Ramsey talked to the D.A. and he agreed that there was enough evidence for an indictment."

Numb inside, Emma ran her fingers along the glass of milk. Her ex-fiancé was in jail for what would probably be a very, very long time.

She'd almost married him. Her life, her mother's life, would have been a total nightmare.

She'd once thought she loved Rob. Now she wanted him in jail.

"What did Cheryl Diamond say?" she asked softly. If the woman had led them to Claire, Lucy would have told her that first. Miller probably would have called her himself.

Sometime over the couple of weeks, Emma had come to accept that her baby sister was gone.

The need to know what happened wasn't about finding Claire anymore. It was about learning to live without her. Learning to live with whatever had happened to her.

She no longer needed hope. She needed closure.

"Cheryl testified today that she met Rob through a website where men have sex with women via webcam, just like we thought. They became close enough for Rob to tell her about you. About why he stayed with you. He told her he first met you at a fund-raiser you and you mother were hosting to raise money for child-safety awareness."

Rob had sex online? In her office? She shuddered, vowing to sterilize everything in the room.

"We were holding a fingerprinting clinic." She forced herself to remember that day. "Statistics show that if there are fingerprints for a missing child, there's a much better chance that they'll find the child during the critical first hours."

"That's right."

"I guess you knew that."

"Yes, but not enough people do. The work you and your mother do is so important, Emma. Please don't stop."

"We won't." Even moving on now, she knew that she wouldn't give up helping others have a chance at a happier ending.

"Anyway, when Rob heard your story, he saw a lawsuit in the making. Apparently he'd been on the lookout for the perfect suit ever since taking a law class in college. In your case, he had no idea if there was proof of wrongdoing, but he knew he could make it look as if there was. When he told Cheryl about you, she wanted in. She got the clerk's job at Comfort Cove's traffic division so she could have access to the evidence box. There was no reason for anyone to trace her to you or anyone who knew you.

"The plan was for Rob to plant some incriminating proof that the police didn't do their job regarding Claire's abduction. Rob told Cheryl that the police never tried to find your sister. That they were so certain the culprit had been Frank that they never looked anyplace else."

He'd heard that from Rose. And Emma hadn't denied her mother's assertions. She didn't know them to be true. But she didn't know that they weren't.

"But Miller went looking for the box before they could get it back into evidence and the whole thing fell apart."

"What was in it for Cheryl?"

"A quarter of the payoff."

Her milk was getting warm. She didn't want it, anyway.

"That's it, then? Another dead end?" The missing box of evidence had nothing whatsoever to do with her sister's whereabouts.

"That's it."

"Well, thank you. For everything."

"I'm not giving up, Emma. I'm not going to quit working on your case."

"Okay."

"I'll be in touch if I hear anything else."

"Thank you." What else was there to say?

"You can call me anytime. If you think of anything else, or just need to talk, I'll be here."

Just like she was there for Tammy.

"Okay, I will. And…if you ever need to vent…about your mother and all…I'm here, too." She needed other women in her life. Her journal said so.

"I might be taking you up on that sooner than you think." The detective's answer surprised her.

"Why? What's going on?"

"We have a lead on the guy who took my sister, the guy who raped my mother. I can't say anything more just yet, but when I can, I'd like it if I could call you."

"I'd like that, too." Emma heard a car out front and, phone in hand, got up to peek around the front window blind.

Chris's truck was in her drive.

Hanging up with Lucy Hayes, tucking the

knowledge of a new friendship inside her heart, Emma prepared to say goodbye to the man she'd been willing to kill for.

CHAPTER THIRTY-ONE

"LET ME JUST SAY what I have to say." Chris didn't even wait for her to invite him in. He had to speak first. Before she thought that anything he said had to do with the possibility of a baby.

He went straight to her living room. Sat on the couch. And looked around. "There aren't any lights on in here."

"I know."

"You don't ever come downstairs without turning on a light."

"I turned them off after I came down."

That meant something. He wasn't sure what. He couldn't get sidetracked.

"I don't know if I could ever give up the sea, Emma. If I was in love with a woman, married to her, and she asked me to quit fishing, maybe I could."

"If a woman loved you back, she'd never ask you to."

"She would if having me out at sea scared her to death. If she couldn't handle it," he stated emphatically. "Anyway, that's not what I came here to say. I'm not my father. But I'm a lot like him in some ways. If I ever fall in love, it will be with one woman until I die. No matter what."

Her eyes were wide as she stared at him. She was standing about a foot away, close enough to touch. But he couldn't reach for her.

"All of that aside, what I really have to say is that I don't believe that fishermen have to be alone. I believe that being married to a fisherman is hard. That a woman has to be strong enough to deal with the lifestyle, but that it could work. All of that stuff I said, about it not working out, it was because I used fishing as an excuse not to risk my heart as my father had done."

"You were afraid?" The odd note in her voice stopped him for a second. Was she smiling at him?

Or crying?

He wished she'd turn on a light.

Or come closer.

"I didn't trust women."

There. He'd said what he came to say. He'd been lying to himself. He hadn't trusted Sara to be true to him. It wasn't the sea that ran her off, it was his inability to commit com-

pletely to her that had done that. His horrified reaction to their possible pregnancy had
stemmed from the idea that Sara would have
his baby and be unfaithful to him while he
was out earning the money that would feed
them. He'd been petrified at the thought of
being so irrevocably tied to a woman that
he'd have to stay with her no matter what she
did behind his back.

"Fishing is all I know," he said aloud.

"Why are you saying this?"

"Because I had to be honest with you."

"Well, thank you. I appreciate that. You're
a good man, Chris. I will never regret having known you."

Her words reminded him of the note he'd
left her that first morning in the hotel across
from Citadel's.

What an ass he'd been.

"You were willing to kill for me."

"I'd have done the same for anyone."

He didn't doubt that. "When I saw what
you were going to do, when I heard the gun
go off, I…" He didn't know what else to say.

"Would you like a glass of wine?"

"Hell, yes."

LEAVING CHRIS IN the living room, Emma
took her time opening a new bottle of mer-

lot, and pouring two glasses generously full, but not so full that she spilled them as she carried them into the other room with trembling hands.

Settling next to him on the couch in the still-dark room, she held a glass out to him. "Here's to truth, Chris," she said, and watched him over the rim of her glass as she sipped.

He tipped his glass and drank.

"I'm not sure why you're here, telling me this, but it doesn't really matter." With no plan, no analyzing or forethought, Emma started to talk.

"I've been keeping this journal." It was her private secret. "More and more I've been looking at it. Reading it."

"When do you have time to read?"

"It's only six sentences long."

"Six sentences?"

She nodded. Feeling tears burn the backs of her eyes, she said, "That day I found Rob in our bed with another woman…I was… empty. I knew I didn't want him in my life for another second, but I didn't know what would be left when he was gone. I didn't plan to keep a journal. I never made a conscious decision to try to work through my thoughts. It just happened. And it helped. Anytime I felt absolutely certain about something, anytime I made a discovery about myself that felt completely true, I'd write it down."

"And you came up with six truths?"

"Yes."

His gaze serious, his eyes glistening with an emotion that took her back to the night she'd first heard him play the piano, he said, "I'd like to read them."

The journal was in the drawer next to him.

She'd held it on her lap while she slept on the couch after Ramsey Miller had dropped her off at home last night.

She'd read it that evening when she'd come home from the doctor's office.

And she'd known that she was meeting her true self.

"We have a lot of things against us," she said. "I have an aversion to the docks, you live on them. I want to be loved by a man who loves me so much that love changes him. My mother will probably hate you. While I have to admit I didn't hate being on the water, or even helping with the catch, I did hate throwing up the whole time we were out there. I'm eleven years younger than you are, and I most definitely want children. As many of them as I can have. But all that aside, I also know, clearly and unequivocally, that

I love you, Chris Talbot. Not only that, I am *in love* with you."

"Is that in your journal?"

"Some of it is."

"The loving-me part?"

"Wait—" she held up her free hand to ward off his questions "—let me finish. I'm not asking you for anything. I'm just telling the truth. You said that age brings experience, which brings wisdom, and that being true, I've gained something really valuable from Rob Evert. I now know the difference between settling and living, and between security and being in love. I didn't love Rob. And I know that now because of how I feel about you."

She could see his eyes shining in the darkness. "I'm afraid of a lot of things, Chris. I'm afraid of the monsters out there who do terrible things to people. I'm afraid of living life without the feeling you bring into it. But I am most definitely not afraid of loving you. I would have killed Rob, without hesitation. And in that moment I wasn't thinking about anything or anyone but you."

"Emma Sanderson, will you marry me?"

"What?"

"I think I was pretty clear."

"Well, yes, but…" She sipped her wine,

clinging to the glass with both hands. He drank, too. But he put his glass down afterward.

"It's not going to be easy. For either one of us. But you're up to whatever challenges life brings you, which means that you have what it takes to keep me on the straight and narrow and I...I just know that when that gun went off, when I saw Evert's arm choking the air out of you, when I thought I might have lost you...every bit of hope I'd ever known went out of my life. I can't live without hope, Emma."

She'd been willing to do that. To give up hope. Even though she'd known that holding on to hope was the one thing she did best. Was it because Chris had become entwined with her hopes?

Hope wasn't just about Claire. It was about all that life held. It was about living.

"You're a wise man, Chris Talbot."

"I'm an old man, Emma. Wisdom comes with age."

"Wisdom comes to those who are willing to open their minds," Emma said. "That's what I tell my students."

"See, I need you as a teacher, Em."

She needed him period. But...

"There's someone I want you to meet," he

said, his gaze warm as he studied her face. "My Aunt Marta and Jim. They're not blood relatives, but they're family, and I know, the second I mention you, they'll be clearing out a space for you in their home, too."

"You think I should live with them?"

Chris laughed. "I just think they'll cling to you—especially Aunt Marta. She needs a daughter-in-law."

Emma smiled. She was overwhelmed, too.

"And there's something else." Chris's voice was serious.

"What?"

"I wasn't ever going to mention this, but, well, I can't bring you into my life without telling you...."

Her heart pounded with fear. Dread. "What?"

"Aunt Marta and Jim knew your father."

She shrugged. "He was a biological fact," she told him. "He was not my father in any true sense."

"I know that." Chris sounded completely certain of that fact. And when he finished telling her what Marta and Jim had told him about her dad, Emma had tears in her eyes. But not for herself.

"My poor mother..." she said, feeling a huge rush of love for the woman who'd sacrificed so much—and lost more. "All she ever wanted was to love and be loved," she said. The age-old desire….

"I just didn't want you to hear something about him and think that it bore any reflection on you."

Emma shook her head. "I already know he has no reflection on me," she said. "I wonder if Mom knew about Kennedy? About what happened to him?"

"Maybe someday she'll be at a point where you can ask her."

"You never know." She smiled sadly. "There might come a day when she asks *you*."

Chris reached for her hand and Emma let him take it. Knowing that they were crossing over into a life that was going to burn all the bridges behind them.

"This isn't just because you think I'm pregnant, is it?" She always had to look on the negative side of things.

"No. At this point, I wouldn't mind if you were, if it meant you'd marry me. I wouldn't know what to do with a journal—except maybe feed it to the fish—but I've spent some long nights on the ocean lately. And had a talk or two with Marta about things I assumed, but never let myself think about.

Until you. You made me ask questions of myself, Em. Even when I didn't want the answers."

"If I hadn't come looking for you after our first night together, and you hadn't assumed that I was pregnant, would you have ever looked me up?"

The shadow on his face was her answer. And her heart sank.

"I'm not sure what I would have done in the end," he said, looking her straight in the eye. "But I know that that night changed me. I couldn't keep my mind on the job. All I kept seeing were your glorious legs and your long dark hair fanned across my pillow."

"So the sex was good."

"It was far more than that. I went to see Aunt Marta before I had any idea that you might be pregnant."

Emma wasn't sure about the significance of that, but she knew he'd just told her something big.

"I might not be as quick as you, Em, but I fought my way through a lifetime of scars to admit to myself that I love you. That the reason everything about me was changing, the reason I needed to ask questions and face the answers, was because I was in love with you, and that love would not let me run from the truth."

Her eyes filled with tears again. Happy tears.

"The reason I wanted to have my say first tonight was so that, if you are pregnant, you won't just think I'm just saying all of this because I have to. I knew when I docked this morning that I was going to ask you to marry me."

"You spent the night on the ocean?"

"I intend it to be the last night I ever spend out there alone."

"You said goodbye." Not to fishing. She knew he'd never leave that—but it sounded as if he'd let go of the idea that life as a fisherman had to be a solitary one.

"Maybe."

"I didn't expect this."

"I know. But I also knew that if I waited to find out if you were pregnant, and you were, and then I asked you to marry me, you'd turn me down for sure."

"Wise man."

"I just understand the woman I love," he said, and then added, "I don't think my father ever did."

She wasn't sure what he meant by that

statement, but she had a feeling that he'd tell her. When he was ready.

"You never answered my question. You aren't going to make me ask again."

She reached in the drawer beside him, pulled out the journal and handed it to him opened to the first page.

"'I want to be loved by a man who loves me so much that that love changes him,'" he read out loud and then looked up at her. "Wow, you hit that dead on."

"I know what I want and I know I can't settle for less than that."

"You're making me nervous."

Shrugging, she nodded toward the book.

"'I want to be brave enough to live life to the fullest,'" he read. "Oh, God, Emma, you're the most courageous human being I've ever met."

"I quake inside just getting up in the morning," she told him because he had to see the bad to really love the good. "Read."

"'I need other women in my life—and their presence is not disloyal to my mother or Claire,'" he read, and looked up again.

Putting her wineglass down, Emma wrapped her arms around her middle. "Growing up, I never had a best friend, or even a particularly close friend. It was always just

Mom and me, on our mission, apart from the rest of the world."

He brushed at the dampness beneath her eyes. "I'm sorry."

"Me, too. I heard tonight that Rob was just with me because he'd been on the lookout for a potential lawsuit that would give him a life on easy street, and I fit the bill. He didn't know anything about what happened to Claire. He just stole the evidence box, or rather, he had one of his bimbos do it, so he could plant evidence that would gain him a win in the lawsuit he was going to force Mom and me to file."

"He'll get his justice, Em. I have no doubt about that. Fate has a way of evening those scores."

Shuddering, she said, "I'm just glad that I had the sense to kick him out before I married him. And that he's in jail."

"But it means you're no closer to finding answers about your sister."

She nodded. "I know. But I'm accepting the fact that we might never know. I lost twenty-five years to Claire's memory. I can't lose any more."

Leaning over, Chris kissed her. Long and slow. Then he sat back, looking down at the leather-bound book he held.

"'I want to have great—'" he broke off, coughed, glanced at her and continued "'—sex with the man I marry. I want to have children.'" He ran number five right in with number four.

And...

"'I want to marry Chris Talbot.'" He read her sixth and final entry—written that evening.

He stared at her and she said, "As soon as possible, please."

"You're pregnant, then?"

"No, sir, I am most definitely not pregnant. I just want to be and I'd like to do it right this time."

He took a sip of wine. "You aren't?" How could he feel so high and so low at the same time?

"No. I heard it from my doctor this afternoon. And I started my period tonight."

"Which gives us about three weeks, give or take your irregular cycle, to get married."

"You think we can wait that long to make love?"

Pulling Emma up against him, Chris picked up her phone from where she'd left it on the table.

"What are you doing?" She let her head rest against his chest as she watched.

"Calling your mother," he said, scrolling

through her speed-dial contacts. "If she's going to hate me as much as you say she will, she'll keep you away from me until we can make it legal."

Laughing, Emma let him make the call.

Rose was going to have to get used to having a son-in-law with a mind of his own.

And a daughter who, while she loved her mother dearly, had to live her own life.

She had a feeling her mother wasn't going to put up much of a fight.

Especially after she met Chris.

After a lifetime of searching, Emma had found her joy.

EPILOGUE

"RAMSEY?"

"Yeah, Luce." Blinking, Ramsey Miller leaned on one elbow in bed, glancing at the laptop computer on the pillow next to him to catch the time.

"They got him, Ramsey!"

He shot up, the cool air hitting his naked chest as he ran a hand through his hair. No need to ask what she was talking about. Not at three in the morning. Lucy had been hot on the tail of her mother's rapist. Her sister's kidnapper.

"They're sure it's him?"

"Yeah. They picked him up tonight on a broken taillight." Ramsey didn't ask how the taillight got broken. He didn't need to know.

Lucy could have done it. He would have.

"We did a DNA swab and it was a positive match with the sample from Mom's rape kit."

It hadn't been called a rape kit twenty-seven years before, but thank God they'd saved the emergency-room evidence.

Pulling a suit out of his closet, Ramsey grabbed a shirt and tie and headed toward the shower. "Have you talked to him yet?"

"No. I was hoping we could let him stew a few hours and—"

"Maybe we should question him together." He couldn't be an official part of any investigation in Aurora. But detectives could sit in on cases outside of their jurisdiction if they were invited to be a guest participant.

He wanted this lowlife almost as badly as Lucy Hayes did. Because they knew for sure he'd taken Allison Hayes.

"I was hoping you'd be able to get here," Lucy said.

"Call the airport and get me on a flight while I jump in the shower."

"Done."

He turned on the shower, grabbed his towel off the rack and slung it over the door for easy access. "Does your mother know yet?"

He thought of Rose Sanderson. Of how she'd spiraled downward before his eyes when she'd heard about Emma's being in danger—even with Emma standing right there.

"No, and I'm not telling her. I need her sober. She's the only witness we have and she might remember something based on what he says."

"Agreed."

The water was hot. Ready for him. But there was one more question. "Has he said anything about your sister?"

"No. He hasn't said a word about anything. He still thinks he's in on resisting arrest for a traffic violation."

"Who's handling the case?" It couldn't be Lucy. Not with her relationship to the victim.

"My captain gave it to Amber Lockengren." Lucy's mentor.

"You okay with that?"

"Yeah."

"You think she'll agree to hold off interrogating him until I can get there to watch?" This was why he lived. To bring down the slime in the world.

"I already asked and she will."

"Good."

"So, I'll see you soon."

"Yeah, text me my flight info."

"You got it." She disconnected.

Tossing his phone on the counter, Ramsey got in the shower—as pleased with life as he got.

* * * * *

Look for the third installment in
this series and find
out what really happened in
Comfort Cove!
THE TRUTH ABOUT COMFORT COVE
is available in January 2013.